# SNOWBOUND IN STARLIGHT BEND

*Riding Hard*

## JENNIFER ASHLEY

JA/AG Publishing

*Snowbound in Starlight Bend*

A Riding Hard Novella

Cover design by Kim Killion

❀ Created with Vellum

# Chapter One

Haley's phone, music, and car died at the same time the world went white.

She plowed into a snowdrift, which sent chunks of snow over the hood of her two-day-old Mercedes AMG, up the windshield and onto the sunroof. Silence blanketed the car as the engine cut, broken only by her startled scream.

There was no blizzard, just a leaden sky with fat flakes of snow coming down without ceasing. Haley had sailed around the corner of the empty highway and hadn't seen the blocking snowdrift until too late.

"Linda?" she yelled frantically into the Bluetooth hooked over her ear. "Can you hear me?"

Dead silence. Panic lingered behind Haley's initial shock, waiting to scoop her up.

No, no. No panic. Panic never helped anything. She'd get out of here and call Linda back, explaining what had happened. If worst came to worst, her car and phone had GPS trackers on them. Someone would find her.

But it might be a long time before she was missed. Dad didn't expect her home until late tomorrow evening—she'd planned to take this quiet road to Sandpoint, stay the night in that lovely town, and drive into Seattle the following day. Now Haley was in this white wilderness, on a back road miles from anywhere, half buried, with no way to communicate. Her car's signal was gone as was her phone's. All dead.

She'd heard stories of people stranded on winter roads for days, with nothing but a bag of chips to keep them nourished until they were found. Her heart pounded with increasing fear. Haley didn't even have a bag of chips, just a half-eaten package of M&Ms. No winter gear, only a coat and gloves that had worked fine during her stay in Chicago, since she hadn't gone outside very often.

Great idea, driving home to Seattle from her business meeting in Chicago by herself. Flights had been cancelled for weather, even private planes grounded, but Haley was going to let nothing stop her from reaching Seattle in time for Christmas. She and her dad spent every Christmas together, just the two of them, had since Haley's mother had left them years ago.

No problem, she'd thought. Haley would

welcome the time alone with her thoughts, to think, to plan. She'd gone to a dealership in Chicago, bought a car she'd had her eye on, and driven off. McKees didn't bother with rentals. And here she was.

It was already bitingly cold. Haley buttoned up her coat and pulled her gloves on, trying not to shiver. Snow covered her front windshield, an opaque blanket of white. The back window was somewhat clear, but that didn't help—it showed her swiftly falling snow and the two deep tire treads her car had made, which were already filling.

All right, so she could sit here and panic, or she could get out, clear the snow off the car, back it up, and make her way to the turnoff she'd seen to a town. Whatever it was called. Something about Starlight.

Haley drew a breath, gripped the handle, and opened the door.

*Thump.* The door made it two inches before it struck packed snow. Haley banged with her shoulder, but the snow was deep and frozen solid, and the door wouldn't budge.

*Shit.* She slammed it closed and crawled across the small car to the passenger side, the gearshift and brake digging into her stomach. She hastily unlocked and tried to open the other door.

*Thump.* This one only opened an inch. Same snow, same problem.

*Crap, crap, crappity crap.*

Sunroof. It was controlled by the car's electrical system, but surely Haley could shove it open with her hands.

Nope. Wouldn't budge. It was quickly being covered with snow as well.

Frustrated, Haley slapped her hands against the thick glass above her, knowing she'd never be strong enough to break it.

Seatbelt buckle. She'd heard somewhere that you could use the metal end of the seatbelt to smash a window if you needed to get out of a vehicle.

The sporty look of this car had called to her from the window of the showroom when she'd passed it. Haley had the money—why not? Now the car she'd loved was trying to trap her, its terrific visibility showing her the snow that would bury her alive.

Haley struggled to bring the seatbelt buckle up and bang it into the driver's side window. She beat on the window with it, but nothing happened. The glass was strong, meant to keep her safe.

"Seriously?" Haley yelled. "I'll tear you apart and sell you for scrap, you stupid pile of junk, if you don't let me out of here!"

Something under the hood hissed, hot water dripping into snow. Not good.

*Hands.*

Two huge hands covered with leather landed on her driver's side window. Haley stared in frozen shock as they slowly slid down the glass.

They were a giant's hands, likely belonging to whatever crazy man lived in the middle of nowhere alone, waiting for city girls like her to blunder into snow banks. He'd haul her out of the car and drag her into this silent landscape, never to be seen again.

The hands returned to scrape off another layer of snow. Then a head, covered except for its eyeballs, bent to peer inside her car. Haley shrieked.

The gloves dragged a wool scarf away from the man's nose and mouth, and his words came to her through the thick glass.

"What the hell are you screaming for?"

Haley's cry died away. The man who looked through the cleared snow had a hard face tanned from sun and wind, and very blue eyes. He had dark hair and was far younger than the madman she'd expected, his features attractive in an outdoorsy way.

He looked nothing like a crazed reclusive killer who trapped young women. But then, what did Haley know? She'd never met a crazed reclusive killer before.

She sat up in her seat, pushing her hair back from her face. "Who are you?"

The man grinned, which lit up his eyes and made him all kinds of handsome. "Your rescuer, honey."

He continued scraping away the snow, digging a trench from the top down to free the door. Finally, he kicked snow and ice from the bottom of the door, grabbed the handle and yanked it open, reaching in with his giant glove. "Come on out of there, sugar."

Haley didn't take his hand. "I don't need to come anywhere. Just push the car out of the snow, and I'll be on my way."

The man straightened up, rubbing a slow finger over his chin. "That's not going to happen. Roads are blocked up behind you. Snowfall's heavy and the plow won't be through until tomorrow morning at the earliest."

Haley's panic returned. "Why not? Surely someone can drive a plow out here." She had no idea—it didn't snow in her native Seattle. They had ice and more rain than anyone needed but never heavy snowfall like this. She'd ignored the snow during her two weeks in Chicago, her work keeping her indoors—the firm she'd been meeting with had provided her a car with a driver.

"Starlight Bend's only got one plow," the man said, his words as slow as his movements. "And it'll be digging out others with more need. So, I guess you're stuck, darling."

Haley's worry made her sharp. "Please don't call me *darling*. Or *honey*, or *sugar*."

The man lifted his hands. "Sor-*ree*," he said. "Sweetheart."

Haley let out a breath of exasperation. "Can you say anything to a woman without adding an endearment to it?"

SNOWBOUND IN STARLIGHT BEND

He paused, as though thinking this through. "Nope."

Haley waited, then let out another noise of irritation when he laughed.

"Let me take you someplace warm," he said as he held out his big hand again. "You'll freeze in this little bitty car."

She couldn't say he was wrong. Maybe the man had a four-wheel drive SUV with the heater running parked around the corner. He'd force through the snow into this Starlight Bend place and Haley could find somewhere to stay. She pictured a cozy B&B with a mountain view and a nice innkeeper bringing her hot tea and pastries.

"Thank you," she said, a bit stiffly. "When you say 'someplace,' you mean the town, right?"

"Sure." The gloved hand didn't waver. "If that's where you want to go."

"All right." She put her hand in his.

Fingers like steel clamped around hers, and she let out another cry as he pulled her straight out of the car. Her feet left the ground and then came back down with a bump.

A deep, hoarse *woof* made her jump. A huge black animal bounded toward them, red tongue lolling, tail wagging. Haley slipped, her high-heeled boots not good for frozen-solid snow, and the man caught her.

Warmth. Strength. Steadiness of the earth as he straightened her on her feet. Haley's lips parted as she looked into eyes the color of a deep lake. Falling snow gathered on his black hair and glittered in the fading afternoon.

"You okay there?" he asked in a voice like deep night.

"Yes." Haley fought for breath as she tried to slide out of his grasp. "Sure."

The man kept hold of her until she was solidly upright then took his hands away. Which was a shame, because it was cold without them on her.

The dog reached them—a black lab mixed with a little of something else. He reared up and planted giant wet paws on the man's chest. The man laughed, tousled the dog's ears, and pushed him back down.

The dog went straight to Haley. Haley held her hands out flat to keep him from jumping all over her tailor-made coat then bent to pat his side and stroke the top of his head. "Yours?" she asked.

"That's Lance," the man said. "Yeah, he lives with us."

The man seemed to approve of her reaction to the dog—probably a lot of people yelped and tried to run when the enormous thing sprang at them. The dog went with the man, both of them big, strong, confident.

"Where's your car?" Haley asked him. She looked around, her hand on Lance's head, but saw no welcome gleam of a vehicle—car, truck, or SUV.

"You think I came through this snowfall in a

car?" he asked, incredulous. "No. I brought Sammy."

"Sammy?" Haley glanced about again. "Is that what you call your four-wheel drive?"

He gave a great guffaw of laughter. "No. I'm Maddox, by the way. Maddox Campbell. And you?"

"Haley McKee." Haley stuck out her hand in a perfect corporate greeting. "Nice to meet you."

Maddox raised his brows at her hand then covered it with his again, the warmth of his grip incredible. "We already sort of shook. Come on. We better get inside before there's too much more of this snow."

He lifted a large cowboy hat from the top of her car, shook the snow off and planted it on his head. Maddox seized her by the hand and started to move off, but Haley held back.

"Wait. My bags ..."

Maddox didn't let go. "Won't have room for them. I'll send someone down here to get them later."

"No, really — I at least need ..."

She managed to break away from him, slipping out of his grasp at the last moment. She nearly tripped but steadied herself as she reached into the car for her briefcase, stuffing the phone and Bluetooth into it. Haley came out of the car, clicking her remote to lock the doors, and clutched the briefcase to her chest.

Maddox studied her doubtfully. "What's in there? Gold?"

"Just my life." Haley slid and stumbled to him. Maddox gave the briefcase a skeptical glance but took her hand again and pulled her along.

They went straight across a field away from the highway, not bothering with the road. Maddox broke a path through the snowdrifts with his long legs, as though he were a walking plow.

Beneath the new dusting of snow was older snow, frozen and packed. Lance scampered over the top of this, running too fast to sink. He dashed ahead, turned to see them a long way behind him, and came tearing back.

Maddox walked as though they strolled through a spring meadow. His stride was long, his grip on her hand firm. Haley struggled to keep up, but he didn't shorten his steps.

She was wet and very cold by the time they reached woods about a hundred feet from the road. The thick trees shielded them somewhat from the snowfall but not from the chill.

Standing patiently just inside the tree line, reins looped around the big saddle on his back, was a horse. A tall, shaggy horse that turned around when he saw Maddox. He was a black-brown color all over except for a large white streak down his face that widened to take in his entire nose. He walked interestedly toward them, ears pricking, brown eyes taking in Maddox and Haley.

Haley wrenched her numb hand from Maddox's. "*That's* your transportation?"

"This is Sammy," Maddox said. "My four-*legged* drive. Best way to get back and forth from town today. What did you think he was?"

"I don't know—some kind of snowmobile?"

Maddox's low laughter warmed the air. He didn't laugh in understanding—he was enjoying himself at Haley's expense.

He caught up the reins and turned Sammy so the saddle's left stirrup was at Haley's side. She backed a few steps.

"Why don't you have him tied up?" she babbled. "Why doesn't he run away?"

"Because he's Sammy," Maddox said as though he considered this a reasonable explanation. "He stays put when I tell him to." He gave Haley a skeptical look. "You ever ridden a horse before?"

Haley wet her lips, which were chapped with the cold. "No."

"You ever *seen* a horse before?"

"Of course I have," Haley answered indignantly. "We have horses in Seattle. My school had a pony club."

"A *pony* club?" Maddox all but snorted. "Like riding lessons for rich city kids?"

"Something like that, yes."

"Were you in this pony club?" Maddox's eyes glinted as though he'd burst into another round of laughter any second.

"Well, no, actually."

"What club were you in? Let me guess. Debate? Computer?"

Haley swallowed. "Chess."

Maddox let the laughter pour free. It made his blue eyes light up and the corners of them crinkle. "You know, sweetheart, I don't think I've ever met anyone like you before. Come on, I'll give you a leg up."

Haley moved to him in trepidation. Riding a massive horse wasn't her idea of safety, but she was getting colder by the minute. If she didn't find a warm place out of the snow and wind, she'd die of hyperthermia.

She bit back a surprised noise as Maddox grabbed her foot and shin and boosted her upward. Haley scrambled to catch the saddle, nearly going off the other side with the momentum. Maddox caught her with a strong hand and hauled her back, settling her on the seat.

Without waiting, he grasped the stirrup, put his own foot into it, and vaulted up behind her.

Warm, hard male landed at her back. Haley struggled to find her breath as Maddox reached around her and took up the reins, enclosing her in a heated space. Warmth radiated from him like a furnace.

"Ready, sugar?" he asked.

Haley gulped air. "Will you stop calling me *sugar*? I'm a CEO!"

"Yeah?" Maddox's voice vibrated through her body. "Well I'm a CWDGAS."

Haley blinked and looked back at him, his strong chest and curving mouth stealing her breath. "What's that?"

"Cowboy Who Doesn't Give a Shit." He let out a sharp whistle to the dog. "Come on, Lance. Sammy, take us home."

## Chapter Two

❧

Haley was beautiful and snooty, probably worked in an office building in a slick high-rise in the middle of a big city—Seattle, she'd said. What she was doing out here, Maddox had no idea. Her coat wasn't anywhere near good enough for Montana winters, and she'd brought no scarf or hat to keep the cold off her head and face.

Maddox unwound his own scarf as Sammy walked along, a long thing his aunt had knitted him. His aunt loved to knit—she invited all her friends over to do it with her from time to time. When Maddox heard needles clacking in the living room, tongues talking over everyone in town, he knew to make himself scarce.

Haley started as the soft wool fell over her chest, but she knotted the scarf at her throat in quick gratitude.

She had hair a cross between brown and blond, natural as far as he could tell. She wasn't thin like the rich young women splashed across the television shows his aunt liked to watch but she definitely kept herself in shape—probably a jogger. He could imagine her on a treadmill, running in a shoulder-baring tank top with shorts that showed her legs all the way up.

Not a bad picture. Maddox enjoyed it for a moment.

The snow continued to fall, the woods darkening with the coming evening. Lance, who wouldn't be worn out until he fell over asleep by the fire tonight, scampered beside them. Maddox slackened the reins until they hung long, letting Sammy have the bit.

Haley shifted nervously. "Don't you need to steer?"

"Nope." Maddox's slow voice was a contrast to her quick speech. "Sammy knows the way."

"You mean you *don't*?"

Her worry was cute. "I've been riding these woods since I was five. Sammy's been doing it almost as long. He knows where he's going."

Haley craned to peer through the trees. "How far is it?"

"Couple miles. We'll be there in no time."

"Where? The town?"

"Town's too far, and you're too cold. We'll go to my house, and you can make some calls from there."

"You live in the woods?" Her voice quavered.

"No, I live on the other side of the woods." Maddox held the reins negligibly in one hand. "You always this inquisitive?"

"Inquis—" Haley stumbled over the word.

"*Inquisitive.* It means you ask a lot of questions."

"I *know* that." Her backside brushed his thighs as she moved in irritation.

"You're surprised a dumb-ass backwoods cowboy knows big words."

"Maybe." Her voice was subdued.

Maddox chuckled. "You're funny, sweetheart. I have a degree in engineering from UC Davis, in case you're interested."

She gave him another startled look over her shoulder. Maddox had a fleeting glimpse of wide brown eyes before she turned away. "Really? Then why are you—"

"Out in the middle of nowhere?" He shrugged. A good question, and one he didn't have an answer to. "I like it here." Sammy turned without prompting, and Maddox gestured with the hand that held the reins. "My house is over there."

They'd come out of the trees to the top of a snowed-over path. Across a white field lay a farmhouse—an old, two-story frame house painted a deep yellow, his aunt's favorite color. *Like summer sunshine,* she always said.

A porch wrapped all the way around it, the railings white to contrast the yellow. Maddox had the joy of painting all those spindles every couple of years. The barn, in traditional red, sat a little to the left of the house.

"Oh, my," Haley said in wonder.

Smoke rose from both chimneys of the house, and a bright wreath decorated the front door. Rolling hills covered in silent snow rose behind the house and barn, stretching to the bulk of mountains on the horizon, visible even on this overcast day.

"Like a postcard," Haley said, enchanted. "It's lovely."

"It's home," Maddox said. Boasting about it did no one any good. "Aunt Jane has some fires going, and knowing her, she'll have plenty of hot things to eat and drink ready."

He sensed more questions bubbling up in Haley, but she managed to tamp them down as Maddox rode Sammy across the field, the snow coming down faster. He halted Sammy at the front porch before he could simply walk on to the barn. "Here's where you get off."

Haley cranked around to stare at Maddox again, clearly having no idea how to climb down.

Maddox dismounted by pushing himself backward off Sammy, who would never dream of kicking him. He wasn't that kind of horse. Lance circled Sammy as Maddox went to Haley, where she waited in the saddle, and hauled her down.

Her body, soft and feminine, crushed against Maddox's. She smelled good, like lemons and fresh air. Her muscles were pliant, curves beneath her clothes. A man could enjoy getting to know those curves.

Haley's hands came to rest against Maddox's chest. Her brown eyes had flecks of gold in them — they also held a lot of anxiety, a woman out of her element and not sure what to do.

Well, she had nothing to worry about. Aunt Jane would thaw her out with coffee, he'd make some phone calls, and they'd get her on her way.

She'd head on to Seattle and Maddox would never see her again. Which would be too bad ...

The front door burst open. "There you are." Aunt Jane skimmed onto the porch in the swift way she had of doing everything.

She was thin, half Maddox's size, and moved like a tornado through a wheat field. When she did her errands in town, everyone scrambled to get out of her way. You always knew where Aunt Jane was by the people flying apart ahead of her.

Haley wrenched herself out of Maddox's arms and nearly slipped again. Maddox casually put out a hand and steadied her.

"How's the storm?" Aunt Jane demanded, her fists on her hips. "Roads blocked? Who is this? Another stray?" Aunt Jane's blue eyes softened as she ran her gaze over Haley, who stood awkwardly next to Maddox. "Aw, you look all worn out, honey.

Maddox, help her inside. Come on now, it's cold. By the way, I picked up that card you asked me to, from the Christmas gift tree at Big Sky Living," she continued as Maddox handed Haley up the porch stairs, making sure she didn't fall again. "Why don't you put away Sammy while I get this poor girl warmed up?" Aunt Jane held out her arm to usher Haley inside. "Do you want coffee or tea, sweetie? I have both brewed up."

———

HALF AN HOUR LATER, HALEY FOUND HERSELF sitting on a comfortable sofa, having shed her coat, boots, and Maddox's scarf, a mug of steaming tea in her hand. She was from Seattle, land of coffee, a beverage she disliked, so she always welcomed tea.

Aunt Jane's last name wasn't Campbell, like Maddox's, but Howard. She was Maddox's mother's younger sister. Maddox's parents had been killed when he was eight, in a small plane crash when they'd been visiting friends in Wyoming. Aunt Jane had moved into Maddox's family's house and taken care of him from then on.

Maddox raised and trained horses, not for racing or rodeos, but to be stunt horses in the movies or TV. His cousins who lived down in Texas were stunt riders, famous ones — Maddox supplied the horses he thought would work well for them. He also helped out kids who didn't have much, teaching them about horses and riding. A real sweetheart, Aunt Jane said. Everyone in town loved Maddox.

Maddox himself came in through the back door in time for the last declaration. He hung up his hat on a hook next to the door and shrugged off his long coat.

"Has she been telling you my life story?" He pulled off his cowboy boots and jammed his feet into sneakers he obviously wore only indoors.

Moving with ease for such a large man, Maddox grabbed a mug from the tray Aunt Jane had brought out and poured himself a huge cup of coffee from the pot on the sideboard. He plopped himself on the other end of the sofa Haley sat on and took a long, noisy sip.

"Ah," he said after he swallowed. "Thanks, Aunt Jane. Cold out there."

Aunt Jane gave Maddox a severe look. "We're trying to reach Haley's folks, but nothing's working. Not her cell phone, not our land lines."

"Happens," Maddox said. "Phones go out around here sometimes, especially in a bad snowfall."

He leaned back, perfectly relaxed, not worried at all that a total stranger was sitting in his house, drinking tea with his aunt, while his aunt regaled her with tales of his childhood.

He also didn't look as though he'd be bothering to go anywhere for a while. Haley cradled her mug, which warmed her fingers, but she couldn't calm herself to the level of these people. To look at them, you'd think nothing was wrong.

"Um—you mentioned going back for my suitcases?"

"Hmm?" Maddox turned his head on the sofa's back and sent her a lazy look from his blue eyes. His hair was dark brown, almost black, strands curled against the flowered chintz of the sofa. "They'll be fine for now."

Haley's annoyance grew. "I can't just leave them out there for anyone to take."

Maddox gave her an amazed look. "Who's going to take them? Don't worry so much."

"Maddox," Aunt Jane said disapprovingly. "She's a guest. Stop teasing her."

The faint smile twitched his lips. "Can't help it. Teasing is what I do. But you don't have to worry. Buddy's bringing your suitcases on his way."

"Who's Buddy?" Haley asked anxiously.

"He helps me out feeding and grooming the horses," Maddox replied without moving. "I texted him to stop by your car and dig out the luggage."

Haley said with exaggerated patience, "*How* will he? He doesn't have a key to the trunk."

Maddox's eyes flickered. "Oh, locks never stopped Buddy." To Haley's alarmed look he said, "But he doesn't steal things anymore. He's gone straight."

Haley sat up, not feeling any better. "If you can text, then may I borrow your phone to let my dad know I'm all right? And to make arrangements to stay in a hotel in town?"

Maddox slipped a phone out of his back pocket. "Be my guest."

Aunt Jane broke in quickly, "You don't want to stay in town, Haley. We don't have any nice places and everyone's full up for Christmas anyway. Besides, it's a long way on horseback when the roads are closed."

"I have to stay somewhere." Haley opened Maddox's text messaging app to find a long row of contacts. For a guy who lived with his aunt in a small town, he knew a lot of people.

Her own phone refused to work at all. When she'd attempted to call her dad, the whole thing had gone dark, and trying to reboot hadn't helped. Her power cord, which should have been in her briefcase, must have gotten tossed into one of her suitcases and was still in the car. Aunt Jane had said she didn't like and didn't use cell phones, so if they had cords here to charge it up, she didn't know which ones would work or even where they were.

Maddox's phone wouldn't connect either but Haley, in hope, tapped in her father's number on the texting line and typed a brief message. When she hit "Send" it said, *Message failed. Try again.*

She tapped the phone once more, and again, and again. She growled in her throat as she ended up hitting it over and over with her finger until Maddox jerked the device out of her hands.

"Come on, now. It's not the phone's fault." He looked it over, as though maybe she'd broken it. "Anyone else you want to try?"

Haley's fingers shook as she pushed back hair that had fallen into her face. Usually she was so well groomed, hair tamed, clothes neat and unwrinkled, everything she needed tucked into specific pockets inside her briefcase. Everything in its place.

Now she couldn't find half of her things, her hair wouldn't stay put, and she was shaking, in spite of the heat of the excellent tea.

Linda—she'd be able to contact her dad for her. "Linda Krantz. Her number is ..." She pressed her hands to her head, trying to think. That was the trouble with modern technology. You didn't have to remember numbers anymore—just start typing a name, up it pops on your list, no phone numbers to memorize. Great, until you didn't have your data and you couldn't remember your best friend's phone number to save your life.

"It's ..." She lowered her hands, eyes stinging with tears. "I don't know. I need my phone, but it's dead. It probably got smacked around too much when I crashed."

"Let me see it." Maddox held out a large, work-hardened hand.

Haley dug through the briefcase at her feet and slapped the useless piece of plastic into Maddox's palm. Maddox held it up in front of his face and tapped it once.

"Yep. I'd say it's busted."

Haley sat on the edge of the couch. "How is that supposed to help me?"

Maddox's eyes softened. "Hey, sweetie, take it easy. I'm just messing with you. It's probably out of power." He got off the sofa and went to a table near the front door. Extracting a white cord, he plugged in her phone and set it on the table. "If it's truly broken, there's a guy in town who can fix it. He can fix anything."

"I thought you were an engineer." If he was going to give her shit, Haley could do it right back to him.

Maddox rumbled a laugh. "Sure, of big things like windmills and mines. Not tiny little cell phone chips. Not with these hands." He held them up and spread his fingers, showing her broad and blunt digits, hard from ranch work. "And my degree was just for school. I found out I'd rather be with horses, not machinery."

"Is that why you live out here in the middle of nowhere?" She'd asked him that already, but he hadn't answered.

Maddox's amusement died. "Everything's somewhere, sweetheart. The back of beyond to you is home to someone else."

Aunt Jane looked disapproving of the whole conversation. Haley got to her feet. "I'm sorry," she said to Aunt Jane. "I'm not trying to be ungrateful. I just want to go home."

Home to her cushy apartment in Seattle, hosting business parties in the few days between now and Christmas. Then Christmas dinner with her dad, the one day of the year that was just about them. Her mom had deserted them a long time ago to be with her boyfriend, and now it was Haley and her dad—Robert McKee, or just McKee as he was called by everyone. He'd be worried.

No, he'd be in back-to-back meetings, lifting his head every once in a while to wonder if Haley would be much longer.

Aunt Jane rose and put her arm around her. "You poor sweetheart. Don't listen to Maddox. He enjoys being a pain in the backside. You are going to stay right here with us—no, don't argue—we have plenty of room, and you'll have a nice cozy bedroom all to yourself. Buddy will bring your things, and when the snow stops, we'll get you on the road. You're lucky Maddox found you. He's really very sweet, when he's not acting like a lummox."

"Nah," Maddox said. "I'm a lummox. But she's right. You're welcome to stay here—I guarantee it's better than anyplace in town where they might only find you a closet to sleep in. Aunt Jane always keeps the place nice for visitors." He picked up a snowflake-shaped card that had been resting on the table. "Is this from the gift tree?"

Aunt Jane rubbed Haley's shoulder. Haley wished the woman wouldn't be so nice, because she was about to collapse in a puddle of aching tiredness, worry, and relief. Easier to argue with Maddox, using the friction he caused to keep her awake and upright.

She'd be all right, Haley told herself severely. She dealt with crises far worse than this running a huge business.

But that was work. This was personal—real life —something Haley wasn't very good at.

"That's it," Aunt Jane said to Maddox, nodding at the card. "Hope you have enough time to get whatever the poor kid wants."

"Gift tree?" Haley asked, curiosity working through her emotions.

"It's become a Christmas tradition," Maddox said. "Kids hang these cards on a tree down at the sporting goods store, we pick one out, and we're that kid's secret Santa. The kids don't have a lot—their parents are out of work or they're farm workers who don't earn very much. At least they all get one nice gift under their tree. I'll pick up whatever this kid— oh, it's Danny Vining—" he read the name, "wants and take it back to the guy who's playing Santa this year."

"Oh, that's nice," Haley said. "What does Danny want?"

Maddox opened the card, which spread into two identical snowflakes. His gaze became fixed, all amusement gone. "Shit," he said softly.

"What?" Haley and Aunt Jane asked at the same

time. They both moved to look over Maddox's shoulder.

In a careful but childish scrawl, the little boy Danny had written what he wanted most for Christmas.

*My Dad.*

# Chapter Three

❦

Maddox's heart dropped into his shoes. Every year since that rich guy, Noah Elliott, had set up the charity tree, Maddox had driven to Kalispell or over to Missoula and bought one of the latest toys or gadgets that the boy or girl he'd chosen wanted.

He knew Danny. The kid was about eleven, in trouble a lot. His mother, who held down two low-paying jobs to make ends meet, didn't have time to deal with a handful like Danny. Maddox helped out when he could by taking Danny fishing or camping, teaching him to ride and work with horses. Danny liked the horses and stayed out of mischief when he was around them.

Haley's hair brushed Maddox's hand as she leaned forward to read the card. "Poor kid," she said. "What happened to his dad?"

"Disappeared a few years ago," Maddox said woodenly. "As in, he blew town without making a secret of it and headed down the highway, never coming back."

"Asshole." Her brown eyes flashed with anger that matched his own.

She didn't elaborate as she took the card, her chest lifting with a long breath.

Maddox had lost his parents and that had been a terrible, terrible time. But at least his mom and dad had loved him to the end, and Maddox felt that love still, twenty years later. Danny's dad had been a total screw-up. He hadn't abused his wife or Danny, thank heavens, but he'd been a shithead who probably wouldn't do Danny any good if he came back.

But every boy wanted his dad. Maddox would have done anything to have his dad and mom come home, say it had all been a mistake, and that they were fine.

"What do I do with this?" Maddox asked, mostly to himself. "Anything I come up with will be a big let down for Danny."

Haley ran her thumb over the card. Her hands were slim, nails trimmed but not decorated in the fancy-ass way women often had them.

"We'll think of something." Haley sounded intrigued.

"So you're staying then," Aunt Jane said to her.

Haley looked up. "I don't have a choice, for now.

Might as well help out. If I can get through on the phone or text I can have my PA find something really nice for him."

*PA.* She had a personal assistant, for crap's sake. "I'll take care of it," Maddox said abruptly.

More anger flashed in Haley's eyes. She held on to the card when Maddox tried to take it back. He tugged. She tugged. For some reason, Aunt Jane was smirking.

Haley didn't let go. "Why don't you want me to help?"

"A gift should be personal," Maddox growled. "Not what your assistant picks up on her lunch hour."

Haley's brows slammed together. She was pretty when she scowled, but Maddox wasn't about to tell her that. "*Your* assistant is bringing my bags," she said. "Are you telling me you never have him run errands for you?"

She had a point, damn it. "Not one like this."

Haley glared at him, her fingers clamped to the card. "We'll give my assistant some ideas, she'll find appropriate things, and we'll narrow down the list. I do it all the time. My dad always loves what we come up with."

"Good for your dad. I bet he's used to gifts from high-end department stores. This is an eleven-year-old boy who picks fruit after school to help his mom make ends meet."

"All the more reason to find him a great present

Something his family would never be able to give him."

Maddox clenched his teeth. She got his blood up, that was certain. "I said, I'll take care of it."

Her scowl remained, a challenge in her eyes. She wasn't going to give in easily.

Maddox was surprised at himself. He didn't usually argue with women. He took them out, bought them dinner, cuddled up with them, and then the two of them went their separate ways. Women didn't want a long-term relationship with a man who was up to his knees in horseshit most of the time, and Maddox wasn't ready to settle down. Or so he told himself.

Haley had both irritated Maddox and made him laugh from the moment they'd met. He'd scared the shit out of her when he'd peered through her snowy car window, which had been funny. Now she was busy pissing him off.

He did not need a rich daddy's girl coming into his small town and telling the backwoods cowboy what to do, and neither did a desperate kid like Danny.

On the other hand—could Maddox justify not letting her help find Danny something truly special because his pride was hurt?

He growled, let go of the card, and said, "Fine. We'll try it your way. I appreciate it." Every word was hard.

Haley folded her arms, which pushed up her

breasts in her clingy sweater. "That is the crabbiest concession I've ever heard. But I'll take it." She sighed and dropped the card to the table. "Not that I'll be able to contact my PA. How do you live without your phones working?"

"Because we know everyone around," Maddox said. "We just go to their houses if we want to talk to them."

"And our phones usually work," Aunt Jane put in. "The snowstorm has knocked out some lines, I guess. Ease off, Maddox. She's stranded and upset. But don't worry, dear." Aunt Jane patted her arm. "I'm making us a nice big supper to take our minds off our troubles."

"Thank you," Haley said, her voice softening. "I truly appreciate all your help." She switched her glare back to Maddox. "*That's* how you show gratitude."

"Don't push it, sweetheart," Maddox said. Movement caught his attention out the back window. "I see Buddy on his way. You make yourself at home, and I'll go tell Buddy he's just been promoted to my PA."

Haley rolled her eyes, but she turned to Aunt Jane, sweet as sugar. "Is there anything I can do to help you, Ms. Howard?"

"You come on in the kitchen with me," Aunt Jane said. "Let the men be cold. And call me Aunt Jane, dear. The whole town does."

BUDDY ASKED MADDOX ABOUT HALEY, CURIOUS after fetching her bags and handing them off to Aunt Jane through the kitchen door.

As the two of them fed and bedded down the horses for the night, Maddox told him about finding Haley and bringing her home. In the morning, more of the crew would be there to take care of the half dozen horses Maddox was currently training and get them some exercise, snow or no snow. Horses didn't know it was the holidays.

"She's a poor little rich girl from Seattle," Maddox finished. "Happy to get the hell out of here as soon as she can."

Buddy grinned at him as they shut the last stall, which happened to be Sammy's. The bay horse leaned his white blaze nose over the partition as though wanting to be part of the conversation. "I take it she's good looking?" Buddy asked.

Buddy was five years younger than Maddox, but heavy drinking that started in his teens plus a few years in prison made him look older, his skin leathery from Montana sun and weather. He was sober now and straight, but his hard living had taken its toll.

"Sure, she's cute," Maddox said with a shrug. Haley got under his hide but he had to admit she was attractive. "Why'd you ask that?"

"Because she wouldn't piss you off so much if she wasn't. You'd be nicer to her if you didn't think she was good looking."

Buddy's eyes twinkled, which only made Maddox more irritated. "What the hell is that supposed mean?"

Buddy shrugged and patted Sammy's nose. "Means it's been a long time since you had a woman."

Maddox fell silent. He could snap at Buddy that it was none of his business, but Maddox had been interfering in Buddy's business since they were kids. Trying to keep him straight and clean. Telling him to come and work for him when no one wanted to hire an ex-con. Buddy could get away with saying things to Maddox other people couldn't.

"Yeah, well," Maddox said after a time. "I doubt anything's going to happen there. She'll be out of here when the roads are cleared, back to her penthouse." He shook his head. "I'm more worried about what I'm going to get Danny."

He'd told Buddy about that too. Buddy nodded. "That's rough. I knew Danny's dad. He could be a total son of a bitch. Kid's probably better off without him."

"I know." Maddox adjusted his hat, bracing himself to leave the warmth of the barn for the blast of cold between here and the house. "But I remember being Danny's age and wishing like hell my parents would come back. I wanted a miracle. I know what he's going through."

"So what are you gonna do?" Buddy asked.

Maddox patted Sammy's neck, saying good night. "Probably take Haley's offer to help me buy him a good gift. It won't compensate, but I gotta get him something."

Buddy's grin returned. "Then I guess you'd better be nice to the rich girl."

"Yeah." Maddox pulled his coat tighter and headed with Buddy for the door. "I feel bad for her, getting stuck out here, but for some reason I can't help sparring with her. She knows how to push my buttons."

Buddy let out a bark of laughter. "I bet she does. Let her push whatever she wants."

Maddox shook his head. "It's nothing like that. Thanks for bringing her bags, though."

"She sure has a lot of them. But women, you know?"

Maddox agreed, though Aunt Jane could go on a two-week vacation with one overnight bag. "Aunt Jane's fixing supper. Want to stay?"

They exited the barn, bending their heads to the wind. "Nah," Buddy said. "But thanks. Mary and Will are expecting me back." His voice warmed as he spoke the names of his wife and three-year-old son. Buddy's reform had come not so much from Maddox helping him out, as it had from the birth of little Will. Buddy had been a changed man from the night he'd held his son for the first time.

"Got it," Maddox said. "Give them my love."

"Will do." Buddy adjusted his hat and moved off down the hill toward his house. The path he'd beaten on the way up was already filling with snow.

Maddox watched Buddy hunker into the wind and march determinedly home before he turned and made his way to his own back porch.

Laughter sounded inside as he reached for the kitchen door. He saw through the glass the warm glow of the room, Aunt Jane glancing from the stove to Haley. Haley had a towel pinned to her waist as an apron and was chopping vegetables on a board. She joined with Aunt Jane in laughing about whatever was the joke.

Her face was half turned to Maddox, her eyes lit, her smile wide. She looked relaxed, her hair pulled into a sloppy ponytail, one hand on her hip, the knife in the other hand resting on the board.

*Yep,* Maddox said to himself, warmth stirring inside him. *There's no denying that Haley McKee is one good-looking woman.*

Too bad that tomorrow she'd be gone, a memory.

*In that case,* his treacherous mind went. *Better not waste any time ...*

---

SNOW FELL AND LIGHT FADED AS HALEY JOINED

Aunt Jane and Maddox for supper at the dining room table. Maddox settled his aunt in her seat like an old-fashioned gentleman, then to Haley's amazement, came around to her side of the table and pulled out the chair for her.

Haley sat, bewildered, then Maddox pushed the chair in. Only then did he take his seat across from her.

Both Aunt Jane and Maddox bowed their heads while Maddox rumbled a prayer over the food. He thanked God Haley hadn't fared worse in her accident and that they were all safe to partake of the food Aunt Jane had cooked.

And she'd cooked a lot. There was a piece of steak waiting on each of their plates, a casserole heaped with roasted potatoes, another of roasted vegetables, a large salad, a bowl of peas with bits of ham in it, fresh baked rolls, and plenty of butter, salt, and pepper.

Haley hadn't sat down at a table with this much food in a long time. Aunt Jane insisted Haley serve herself first, as their guest. Haley scooped out a few vegetables and a forkful of salad under Maddox's sharp gaze.

"You have to eat more than that," he said. He waited for Aunt Jane to dish out her own food then piled his plate high, his steak disappearing under a mound of green, white, and red. "Here, have some potatoes."

Haley held up her hand as he thrust a steaming

spoonful at her. "I really shouldn't have too many carbs."

Maddox barked a laugh and Aunt Jane smiled. "I was raised on carbs," Maddox said. "Hasn't hurt me. So was Aunt Jane. She's tough as a nut."

True, Maddox didn't have any fat on him and Aunt Jane had wiry strength. If they ate like this every night, their metabolisms must be superhuman. Aunt Jane looked like she could run a few miles, wrestle a bear, and then waltz home to prepare another gargantuan meal.

Haley loved potatoes. Her mouth watered at the pile of oven-roasted spuds, glistening with hot oil and dusted with rosemary. "Well, maybe just a little."

Maddox dumped the large mound onto her plate then dropped the spoon back into the casserole dish with a clatter.

Haley sliced a tiny piece from her steak and took a bite. She didn't eat much beef, and she stopped in surprise when the meat nearly melted in her mouth, tender and smoky, with a bite of salt.

"This is good, Aunt Jane," she said, trying not to sound too surprised.

Aunt Jane looked modest. "Thank you, dear."

Haley glanced at the windows, which were black now, the winter day short. Snow slapped against the panes not sheltered by the porch, white grit in the darkness.

"It doesn't snow in Seattle," Haley said wistfully. "Drizzly rain and mist, but no snow."

"Well, we get all kinds of it here," Aunt Jane said. "And sunshine like you wouldn't believe in the summer. It's a beautiful place, Starlight Bend. You'll see."

Sounded like they expected her to stay a while. Haley hoped her dad wasn't getting too worried.

But it was only seven-thirty, which meant six-thirty in Seattle. Dad was probably still in the office, going over new contracts, talking to the people Haley had gone to Chicago to butter up. He wouldn't miss Haley until well into the next evening, maybe even the day after—he'd figure Haley would want some time off to rest from her trip.

The thought that she wouldn't be missed right away gave Haley a strange, lonely feeling.

"What do you do here when you're snowed in?" she asked brightly. "If you can't go to town until the roads get plowed, how do you get groceries and things?"

Aunt Jane looked cryptic. "Oh, we manage."

Maddox pinned Haley with a blue gaze at the same time he surreptitiously slipped Lance a chunk of steak. "We play checkers and drink sarsaparilla."

"No, we do not," Aunt Jane said sternly. "You can stop that right now, Maddox Campbell." She turned kind eyes to Haley. "We enjoy ourselves quite well. Snowbound days help us come together as a community. In fact, our guests should be arriving soon."

Haley blinked. "Guests?"

Maddox grinned, the smile lighting up his eyes and filing off his hard edges. "Sure. What we do when we're snowbound is have a snowed-in party. Should be one hell of a night."

## Chapter Four

They came on horseback, snowshoes, and cross-country skis. Those who lived closer, like Buddy and his wife, risked hiking on foot, beating a path through the snow.

Haley had never seen anything like it. She'd hosted plenty of parties in her big apartment or at her father's house, but most of those were business-oriented, time to get clients and partners relaxed so they'd view Haley and her father as people and not simply names on a contract. Guests at Haley's parties dressed up and were on their best behavior. Even her occasional gatherings for close friends involved martinis and catered finger food.

At least thirty people poured into Maddox's house, from all walks of life. Cowboys and their ladies in sheepskin coats, men in plaid flannel with caps, everyone in boots and scarves, gloves or mittens. They unwrapped themselves in the large space inside the back door, the racks filling with outerwear of all colors and shapes.

Some had brought beer; one couple, champagne; others carried in covered plates of cookies and pie, cake and pastries. Aunt Jane welcomed them all, while Haley stood by in astonishment.

Maddox stepped next to her, a warm bulwark between her and all the strangers. "This is Haley," he told those staring in frank curiosity. "She got stuck in the snow. Least we could do was have a party."

His friends and neighbors cheered. "Hi, Haley!" they yelled. Their wives and girlfriends eyed her pink cashmere sweater and black pants the way women often checked out another woman's clothes —part assessment of how it looked on her, part envy, part wondering where they could find something similar.

The crowd was welcoming, friendly, interested. But even as she joined conversations and asked questions, Haley knew that if she hadn't been championed by Maddox and Aunt Jane, she might not have been as readily accepted. These two seemed to be trusted and respected. Pillars of the community, her dad would call them.

Lance circled the crowd, well known to everyone. He got plenty of attention, plus all the tidbits he could finagle. Haley was a little alarmed about what went into the dog's mouth, but he seemed a healthy, happy animal.

Everyone, of course, wanted to know how Haley

had become stuck in the snow bank, and she had to explain how her great idea about driving home from Chicago had turned not so great. They were sympathetic, glad she hadn't been hurt.

Haley didn't mention that she'd purchased her car outright for the trip, wiring the money to the dealership from her bank account in Seattle. The salesman, who'd thought he'd have a dismal day because of coming storms, had practically done cartwheels.

She closed her mouth over telling Maddox's friends the name of her family business. They might not have heard of it this far off the beaten track, but under her direction, the McKee brand, which had its roots in the lumber boom of the nineteenth century, had expanded a long way. Not that she wasn't proud of her accomplishments, but she didn't want to *be* that accomplishment tonight.

At the moment, she hungered to just be Haley, the woman who liked dogs and long walks in the Seattle mists, drinking tea with her dad, jogging along the waterfront, and unwinding with her friend Linda in their favorite wine bar.

Soon she'd go back to her office where things hummed along at a rapid place and she'd forget all about these friendly people, Aunt Jane and her simple but good cooking, Lance the goofy dog, and a handsome cowboy named Maddox.

THE PARTY DIDN'T BREAK UP UNTIL AFTER TWO. Haley, exhausted from her long drive, her accident, the ride on Sammy, plus all the food she'd eaten, drifted off to sleep on the sofa while everyone talked and laughed around her. Lance parked himself in front of the couch as though guarding her.

Haley was drowsing in a place of warm darkness when she felt herself being lifted. Strong arms closed around her and a hard chest cradled her safely.

In silence Maddox carried her up the stairs. It was quiet now—the guests had gone. Only Maddox's tread and Lance's paws scrabbling on the wooden steps broke the silence.

Maddox carried Haley into a room that smelled of clean linens, and laid her on a bed. When Haley stretched out her arms, her fingers touched the edges of the mattress. She couldn't find the energy to move more than that.

Her high-heeled boots loosened then disappeared from her feet. Stockings followed, ankles held by strong hands that caressed warmth into her body.

Maddox rubbed his thumbs over her feet, then released her. Haley watched him through eyes she couldn't open more than a slit.

He dragged in a breath and let it out in the quiet then draped sheets and quilts over her, smoothing them down.

Haley found herself in a warm cocoon, more comfortable than she'd been in a long, long time.

Maddox's hand drifted to her forehead. As she closed her eyes, she felt heat brush her and the soft press of lips on her hair.

"Sleep tight, Haley McKee," he said, his voice a whisper.

Haley couldn't summon the strength to answer him. She lay still, her body tingling as he kissed her hair one more time. When he pulled away, the sudden cold was difficult to take.

"Come on, Lance," he rumbled.

Lance made a quiet whine, then Haley heard a thump and grunt as the dog lay down, the tags on his collar clinking.

"All right then," Maddox said in exasperation. "Stay there."

He walked out, closing the door all but a crack. Haley smiled. He'd made sure that Lance could get out when he wanted to leave. Only someone who understood dogs would do that.

It was her last thought before sleep consumed her, filling her mind with dreams of a tall cowboy rescuing her from the snow, carrying her away in his arms, and laying her down with kisses of fire.

———

HALEY JUMPED AWAKE WHEN HER PHONE GAVE A three-toned *ping*.

She shoved her hair out of her face, blinking in the faint daylight. White-painted furniture covered

with chintz fabric and cushions met her gaze, along
with a bookcase stuffed with books and knick-
knacks, a dresser filled with old-fashioned toiletries,
and a white-painted table in a niche, perfect for a
laptop. Paintings of landscapes and children holding
flowers decorated the walls.

Her three suitcases rested next to a narrow door
that probably led to a closet. Haley was still dressed,
her sweater and slacks feeling limp and fusty, and
she longed to leap up, shower, and pull on fresh
clothes.

Her phone pinged again. Haley scrabbled for her
briefcase that had been placed on the rocking chair
and dragged out her phone, which was fully
charged now.

The text was from Linda, who'd been her friend
since they'd discovered they had a crush on the same
guy in high school. They'd bonded when he'd
decided to go out with a girl who was already a
model and made it clear he didn't like eggheads.
They'd commiserated and become fast friends.

*You okay?* Linda wrote. *Where are you? We're getting
worried.*

Haley's thumbs busily moved in response. *I'm
fine. In Montana. Tell my dad I'm all right.*

The screen indicated Linda was typing back,
then, *Montana? Where? In a cabin? A snowdrift?
Your car?*

Haley grinned as she sent back: *At a ranch house*

*near a place called Starlight Bend. Nice people helping me. A cowboy and his aunt.*

The phone was quiet for a long time. Haley imagined Linda, her black hair perfectly coiffed, plucked brows over deep brown eyes arching as she studied the phone. Then her coffee-colored fingers dancing over the keyboard.

*Cowboy? Is he hot? Or chew tobacco and spit?*

*Hot,* Haley texted. *Definitely hot.*

The reply came right away. *You need to call me. I can't get through except texting.*

*I will when I can. Tell Dad I'm okay.*

More waiting, then, *OK. Then we are so going to TALK.*

Haley sent back a smiley face.

She closed the app, relieved. A quick test showed Haley she still couldn't call out or text her dad, but Linda would contact him, Haley knew. Haley liked to always make sure Dad knew where she was whenever she could—she did *not* want him to go through what he had when her mother had disappeared.

Weird how the cell service was so arbitrary, as though something in the air influenced it. Maybe that was just the price of living in such an isolated place.

For now … A glance out the window showed her it was still snowing. Haley doubted her car would be dug out today. She would have to stay longer, a thought that made her heart warm.

She stopped, stunned. She was *happy* she couldn't get out of this place and back home to bustling Seattle? Haley loved Seattle, every rainy minute of it.

She heard Lance barking below and saw Maddox stride outside into the snow, Lance leaping after him. Maddox headed around the house toward the big red barn, walking like he had all day and nothing to worry about. He whistled to Lance and patted the dog when he ran close.

Maddox didn't look up at the house, only strolled on, white snow settling on his black cowboy hat. Haley's heart burned. She craned to watch him until he disappeared under the shelter of the barn, then she was sorry she couldn't see him anymore.

She sat back down on her bed with a thump, disquiet, excitement, and feelings she thought she'd never experience again welling up in her.

She had a crush on the arrogant cowboy, Maddox Campbell.

*Well, hell.*

---

MADDOX KNEW WHEN HALEY DESCENDED THE stairs and made for the kitchen. There was a change in the air, a change in his awareness. That, and Lance barreled out the kitchen door right into her.

"Hey, there." Her voice softened a long way as she greeted the dog. "Good morning to you."

Haley liked dogs. Big point in her favor. Once she lost her fear of horses, she'd like them too.

Wait, what was he talking about? She wouldn't stay around long enough for him to teach her to enjoy riding horses. Haley McKee would be back to her billion dollar business real soon. He wondered if she'd mention who she actually was before she went. Kind of rude of her to leave that part out last night.

Haley walked into the kitchen with Lance pinned to her side. She sniffed and said, "Mmm. Smells good, Aunt Jane."

"Just some pancakes and bacon and eggs," Aunt Jane said modestly. "Nothing special."

"I'll take it." Haley was all smiles as she seated herself at the kitchen table. Lance sat next to her, ready in case a piece of bacon escaped and sailed his way.

Haley had put on jeans this morning—slim, tight designer jeans, made for looking good on a casual lunch date, not riding across snowy country.

Aunt Jane dished out food then joined them. "Sleep well?" she asked Haley.

"I did, yes." Haley sounded surprised. "Better than I have in a long time."

Haley caught Maddox's eye and looked quickly away, but she didn't flush, barely acknowledged him. Did she remember him bending down and kissing her good night? At least on the top of the head. Was she mad at him for that? Or did she care?

Likely she hadn't noticed. She'd been far gone toward sleep.

"Feel up to going into town?" Maddox asked her. "To get your phone looked at?"

Haley stopped with an egg-laden fork halfway to her mouth. "The roads are cleared already?" she asked in hope.

"Aren't you cute?" Maddox chuckled. "Nope. Still blocked. I mean, feel up to going into town on Sammy?"

Her expression turned to one of trepidation. "I don't know. Is *he* up to it?"

"He likes you," Maddox said. "He told me," he added with a straight face. "I'll take another horse, and we'll go together."

The eggs started to fall off the fork. Lance edged forward. "Me ride alone?" Haley asked worriedly.

"Easier for Sammy if we don't ride double. You'll be fine."

The glob of eggs fell to the edge of the table. One second they were there, the next, gone. Lance blinked in all innocence, though he had tiny dabs of yellow on his whiskers.

Haley studied her empty fork, frowned, and scooped up more eggs. "I guess I can try," she said.

Now why was Maddox disappointed she didn't argue with him? He realized he kind of liked arguing with her. Her eyes sparkled and her face flushed when they did, and she liked to push herself up to him, her curve of breasts an inch from his chest.

Haley went back to eating. Lance licked the evidence off his whiskers and settled back down to wait and watch.

Maddox would have to come up with more things for them to fight about, he decided, before she disappeared and never came back. He could think of one or two really good things already.

———

"I'M GOING TO FALL OFF." HALEY CLUTCHED THE horn and back curve of the saddle as Maddox instructed while she waited for him to give her a leg up.

*Cantle*. The back part was called a *cantle*, he'd said. As though remembering that would keep her aboard.

"No, you won't," Maddox said. "You did fine yesterday."

"Because you were holding on to me."

That had been nice. His bulk had surrounded her, his warmth cutting the sharp cold.

Maddox didn't look as though the memory was a happy one. "This time your training wheels are off. You'll be all right."

Lance sat and watched all this with interest, his tail furrowing patterns in the snow.

Maddox grabbed Haley's ankle and shin and boosted her up. Today Haley's jeans made mounting a little easier, as did the cowboy boots Aunt Jane had lent her. Aunt Jane's feet were a little bigger than Haley's, but Aunt Jane had stuffed newspaper into the toes and declared they'd be fine.

Haley had donned a thicker sweater and a padded jacket Aunt Jane had found for her. Much better protection from the cold than her light coat. A knit hat jammed over Haley's head kept the wind's nip from her ears.

Maddox pushed Haley upward, then grabbed her around the hips and hauled her back when she started to go over Sammy's other side.

"You're supposed to sit *down*," he growled. "What kind of weird-ass saddles do they have in Seattle?"

"I don't ride in Seattle, so I don't know," Haley said loftily. "And you push too hard."

"Yeah, yeah, blame it on the hard-ass cowboy."

Haley frowned at him. "You have the biggest chip on your shoulder. I'm not some rich city bitch condescending to speak to the country folk." She calmed a little. "Your aunt would never let me even if I wanted to."

"Aren't you?" Maddox's smiles were gone. "When were you going to tell me you're Haley McKee of McKee's Lumber and Hardware, with giant stores all over the west? Did you come here to scope out a new place? To drive all our mom-and-pop stores out of business?"

Haley's mouth hung open, her face frozen, which had nothing to do with the continuously falling snow. Her heart froze too.

Maddox looked furious. Haley felt a stab of dismay. She hadn't wanted to talk about her family's business. People treated her differently when they knew her background, and she was enjoying being plain Haley.

"Of course not," she managed. "I was taking a shortcut, like I said. Heading for Sandpoint."

"Starlight Bend isn't a shortcut to anywhere. Have you told my aunt about this? Or are you too chicken-shit?"

"I did tell your aunt," Haley said quickly. "About being *that* McKee, I mean. Yesterday, when I was helping her make dinner."

Maddox scowled. "She didn't bother to tell *me*. I looked you up. You have your own Wikipedia entry."

She did. Her PA had made sure of it.

"I promise I didn't come here to do anything but drive through," Haley said, not liking how he was looking at her. "We're not planning to expand into small towns. The market studies say it's not feasible."

His anger made his eyes dark. "So you're staying out not because you care about ruining local economies but because you can't make any money?"

Haley firmed her lips. "That is *not* what I meant. I take a lot of factors into account, like whether local people would lose everything they'd worked for. I don't slam stores down without careful thought. Besides, I'd never heard of Starlight Bend until I got stuck here."

"Well, make sure you forget all about it when you're gone."

"Oh, I will. I will. Now, let's get to town so I can fix my phone and find a way out of here."

"Fine," Maddox said curtly.

He slapped Sammy on the rump and the horse jogged forward a few steps. Haley found her world bumping, her feet coming out of the stirrups, and then she was sliding off, arms flailing.

She landed flat on her ass in the snow. Sammy stopped and turned around, lowering his head to make sure she was all right.

Maddox's booted feet stopped right beside Haley. He hauled her up, eyes worried, his arms going around her in the process.

Haley looked up at him. Maddox stilled and looked down at her. They were so close the snowflakes couldn't squeeze between them.

They stared at each other while snow fell, both horses waited, and Lance's tail thumped.

Then Maddox closed his arms firmly around Haley and kissed her hard on the mouth.

# Chapter Five

Sweet taste of a woman. Haley rested her hands against his chest, unmoving, as her lips parted and her tongue licked spice into his mouth.

Maddox's heart thumped so hard he couldn't hear anything, not that there was much to hear. In the silence of the barnyard, he could stand and kiss Haley, unaware of everything but her mouth, her heat, her body against his. She might be ultra-rich and unattainable, but she was one hell of a good kisser.

Haley made a little noise in her throat, which sent his temperature high and made his body rock hard. He had the sudden vision of her with him under his sheets, the room hot with their lovemaking, she giving him a languid smile. She'd brush her fingers across his face, then pull him down to her to drown in her warmth.

Back in the real world, Haley's nose was cold

against Maddox's cheek, her mouth seeking, her hands sinking into his coat and pulling him closer. She wasn't shoving him away. She wanted the kiss, sinking into his embrace and giving him a deep kiss in return.

Maddox firmed his hands on her back, getting lost in her. Her mouth held heat, her body lithe as she swayed against him. Her tight breasts, curved hips, and strong legs pressed him through their coats.

The kiss gave him everything he needed, her lips smooth and warm, her body supple under his hands. Their biting words floated away on the wind, their anger's power dying as they communicated in a much more basic way.

Lance smacked into Maddox's thigh. Maddox stumbled, his mouth bumped Haley's, and she pulled hastily back. Her eyes were wide, brown and gold, lashes flecked with snowflakes, her parted lips red.

Lance wagged his tail hard. He was looking past Maddox at Buddy, who was on his way up the path toward them.

The man grinned hard, which meant he'd seen Maddox kissing Haley. Lance had broken them apart in time for Buddy not to have to shove his way past them. *Good dog.*

"Morning," Buddy sang out. He paused as he reached them. "Need a leg up?" he asked Haley.

"I've got it," Maddox said abruptly, but at the

same time, Haley said, "Would you mind? Maddox keeps throwing me off the other side."

Buddy's mouth quivered as he moved to Haley's side. Maddox would have to kill him later.

Buddy wrapped his arm around Haley's leg before Maddox could object, and had her up and safely in the saddle in the space of a moment. Haley landed solidly on the seat, sending Maddox a look of triumph.

Buddy adjusted the stirrups then waved a hand at her thanks and discreetly walked on toward the barn. Maddox positioned Haley's feet in the stirrups, trying not to enjoy the firm feel of her calves.

"You'll follow me," Maddox said, mounting his horse, a tall gelding with a thick black coat. "Just hold on to the reins and let Sammy have his head. He knows what to do. He won't spook or bolt. Lance, stay here and take care of Aunt Jane."

Lance sat down, looking disappointed, but he stayed. Maddox pulled his horse in front of Sammy, who waited patiently for him to pass.

"What's your horse's name?" Haley's voice behind him sounded strained. Regretting the hot kiss? Or embarrassed by it? Maddox's lips still tingled.

"Boone," Maddox said as he led the way to the path to town. "He was a stunt horse. Retired now. Sammy was the same."

"What kind of horses are they?" Another question to fill the space. "I've never seen any this shaggy."

Maddox patted Boone's neck, his glove sinking into the wiry fur. "All horses have long hair in the winter. If you've only seen horses in shows or on TV, they get clipped for that, regardless of the season. Up here, we let them keep their natural coats in winter."

"Oh." Haley sounded fascinated. "I never knew that." He heard her pat Sammy. "I like them with long hair."

Maddox did too. He'd never admit it, but he loved burrowing his bare hands into his horses' warm winter coats.

Their conversation didn't so much drift into silence as cut off abruptly. Maddox couldn't think of a damn thing to say to her, and Haley ceased asking questions.

Maddox didn't regret the kiss at all, no matter what she thought about it. He'd do it again. In fact, he *would* do it again, as soon as he could. Haley would disappear into her world soon enough, but not before Maddox tasted her once more.

If it led to nothing, then it didn't. If it did—well, he'd work that out later. Maddox had learned a long time ago to live from day to day. Don't anticipate the future; don't hold so tight to the past that you can't walk on.

It was five miles over the fields to Starlight Bend, ten by road. Maddox led Haley along paths he'd known since he could walk, through stretches of woods and open ground, the mountains a constant backdrop.

The town nestled on the edge of a lake, which was iced over now, but in the summer, the lake was deep, deep blue, as though sky and water melded. Mountains towered to the north and west, Starlight Bend in a bowl of beauty. Summer saw the lake full of boats for fishing or just gliding on the water; winter brought ice fishing and snowmobiles.

Maddox rode down into the town, the residents moving around briskly, snow never slowing them down. There was the Lakeside Cafe run by Becky Smith, who made a mean breakfast and killer pies. The scent of fresh-roasted coffee drifted in the air, making Maddox's mouth water.

The bar everyone called Stan's that overlooked the lake was a fine place to hang out with friends after a long day. The sporting goods store, Big Sky Living, where residents of Starlight Bend bought their fishing and hiking gear, could be seen in the distance, dominating the skyline. Lights that were strung up every Christmas hung glittering in the dim winter morning, twinkling like fireflies.

Cars crawled through the main street that had been somewhat cleared, though side streets were still blocked with the snow that continued to fall. A little snow never kept residents of Starlight Bend down for long. The weather was overcast and misty, sending gloom over the town, but when the sun

finally came out again, Starlight Bend would glitter
with a diamond hue.

Maddox lifted his hand to those they passed,
calling greetings. The few who'd met Haley at the
party last night included her in their good-mornings.
More than one person was on horseback, that being
a handy way to get around in heavy snowfall.

Riding horses through town was so common
here that the store Maddox headed for had hitching
posts in the front. Andy Baldwin ran a fixit shop,
simply called Andy's, where he repaired everything
from refrigerators to the latest handheld gadgets. He
had an uncanny knack with electronics and
mechanics that no one could match. If something
broke in Starlight Bend, Andy could fix it.

Maddox dismounted, clipped lead ropes to the
halters his horses wore with their bridles, and tied
the ropes with quick release knots. Then he went to
help Haley down.

She came off Sammy stiffly, her arms going
around Maddox to steady herself. She flushed as he
set her on her feet and quickly stepped away
from him.

Maddox hid his frown and led the way into the
shop. He noticed Haley looking around in bewilderment, which was what most people did the first time
they came in here.

Every inch of floor space was covered with
shelves that reached high overhead, and every shelf
was piled with every device ever made. Microwaves,

toaster ovens, toasters, butane stoves, electric can openers, coffee makers, coffee pots, mixers, computers, monitors, keyboards, motherboards, CD players, cassette decks, turntables, and radios and consoles that hadn't been used since Maddox's grandmother's childhood. All were in a jumble on the shelves, dusty five-and-a-quarter floppy disc drives next to the latest versions of tablet computers.

Of Andy there was no sign, but that didn't worry Maddox. He was in here somewhere.

Haley gave Maddox a look of amazement, then she started wandering around the shelves. The gadgets were strewn about in various states of decomposition—Andy routinely harvested old devices to fix new ones. Wires spewed from metal and plastic, screws and bolts lay haphazardly, computer chips of all sizes and colors were gathered into piles.

Maddox peered down the labyrinth and cupped his hands around his mouth. "Hey, Andy!"

"I heard you." A deep voice came out of the back, like a bear waking from hibernation.

Andy kind of looked like a bear too. He lumbered from his office, a cubbyhole buried in the back of the store, a giant of a man with the build of a wrestler and a shock of dark brown hair the same color as his trimmed beard. His large hands, which dwarfed every one he shook, could manipulate the tiniest pieces of metal with the delicacy of a master jeweler. Andy was ten years older than Maddox and had been interested in what made things work ever since Maddox could remember.

"How you doing, Maddox?" the big man asked. He switched his gaze to Haley and became admiring. "Hey now, what's a good-looking thing like you doing with a loser like *him*?" Andy gave her a friendly grin. "Ditch his ass, honey, and I'll show you the town."

Maddox expected Haley to bristle but she only smiled politely. "I think I've already seen it," she said.

Andy roared with laughter, the sound rattling the air. "I like her. Yeah, Starlight Bend isn't a metropolis, but it's a nice little place." He switched to Maddox, became businesslike—well, as businesslike as Andy ever was. He'd turned his hobby into his profession and never looked back. "What you got for me today?"

"Phone." Maddox held out his hand to Haley, who reluctantly placed her smartphone into his palm. "Haley's doesn't work, and she wants to get in touch with her folks. Our land line is down, and my cell phone won't do anything but text."

"Yeah, snow is messing with a lot of things. My phone's out too and I lost power for a while. I heard Trevor Jones and his wife got stuck in their SUV all night, so I'm guessing there'll be another little Jones coming along next fall." Andy gave a deep laugh and reached for the phone.

Haley watched worriedly as he turned it around

in his big hands. "Won't fixing it violate the warranty?" she asked. "You don't have to repair it—I can always pick up another one when I get home."

Andy shrugged, his eyes on the phone. "Why throw something away when you can fix it easy? Wasteful. Come over to my workbench, honey. I'll see what I can do."

Haley threw Maddox a look of trepidation. Maddox ushered Haley in front of him, leaning down to say to her, "He might not look like it, but Andy's a genius."

"Thanks," Andy rumbled. "I think."

His workbench was nailed-together two-by-fours with a plywood top. It was filled with wires, screws, screwdrivers, pliers, saws from tiny to huge, hammers, files, washers, bolts, and various metal bits Maddox couldn't identify.

Andy seated himself on a stool and popped the back off Haley's phone. He did it without any effort whatsoever—one moment it was in a single piece, the next, the phone's innards were exposed.

Andy swung a magnifying glass over the insides. "Computers are just electronics with switches that turn on and off. Once I figure out which switches won't go on and off, I'll have it fixed."

Haley chewed the corner of her lip as though ready to snatch the phone away and run. Too bad there was nowhere to go.

"Hmm," Andy said.

"What?" Haley asked nervously.

Andy looked up with a start, as though he'd forgotten they were there. "Why don't you two go out shopping or something? Then have lunch. I'll have this finished up by the time you get back."

Without waiting for an answer, he returned to his study of the phone, blanking out the rest of the world.

Maddox indicated Haley should follow him out. The cold hit them as they exited the stuffy shop, the horses waiting patiently. Sammy's rope had come loose from the post, but the horse hadn't moved an inch. He'd taken the weight off one leg to rest, his eyes half closing. Any moment now, he'd yawn.

Maddox showed Haley how to fold the rope in her hand to lead Sammy—everything in town was close to Andy's, so they wouldn't need to ride.

"Why didn't you bite Andy's head off when he called you honey?" Maddox asked curiously. "I thought that riled you up."

Haley sent him a serene look around Sammy's nose. "I've learned to be patient with people's quirks when I need to work with them."

"Huh." Maddox adjusted his hat against the wind. "Didn't notice you adopting that policy with me. Why's that?"

Haley's brows came together and her mouth turned down. "I don't know. I guess you *rile* me. Besides, I'm not working with you."

"No, I just saved your ass from spending the night in the snow."

"I know." Haley gave him an acknowledging nod. "You still rile me, as you say. Like you're doing it deliberately."

"Well, you're no sweet princess, darlin'. You expected me to kowtow to you the minute I met you."

She scowled at him. "Were you expecting me to go all gooey-eyed and say, *Ooh thank you for rescuing me, my knight in shining armor?*"

She said the last in a high-pitched, girly voice that made Maddox want to laugh. "It's dewy-eyed," Maddox said. "Not gooey-eyed."

"Well, I'm not going dewy-eyed over you either."

"Good." Maddox said firmly. "I'm glad we know where we stand."

"I so can't wait to get out of this town," Haley muttered. She caught sight of the log-built sporting goods store at the end of a long street. It would be busy this morning as it was the biggest place in town to shop—Maddox guessed a lot of Christmas presents were being purchased inside.

"Can we swing by there?" Haley asked, pointing. "I'd love to see the gift tree. It sounds like a cool idea."

"Sure." Maddox turned away from it, heading up Second Street.

Haley's footsteps quickened behind him, though Sammy plodded at the same pace. "You know you're going in the opposite direction, right?"

Maddox didn't stop. "There's no horse parking at

Big Sky Living. We have to leave them at the livery stable."

"A livery stable?" Haley's voice showed interest again. "You have a real livery stable in this town?"

"Sure do, ma'am," Maddox said. "And on a day like today, I bet it's almost full up."

An enterprising woman, Liddy Talbot, and a friend of Aunt Jane's—who wasn't?—had taken over an abandoned stable in the middle of town and turned it into a boarding place for local horses. She took care of and trained horses for those who didn't have time, and she provided stalls for those who rode to town and didn't want to leave their horses exposed to traffic.

Liddy met them in the yard behind her office. She greeted Boone and Sammy by name, and one of her helpers, who happened to be Danny this morning, came to grab their reins.

Danny glanced shyly at Maddox and then at Haley. After Maddox introduced Haley, he glanced at her and touched his finger to his lips. Danny wasn't supposed to know that Maddox had drawn his name on the gift tree.

Danny was a wiry kid, eleven going on twelve. The teachers at school shook their heads over him but around horses, Danny was calm, quiet, and smart. He didn't say much, but he always had a hello for Maddox.

Haley was subdued when Maddox led her away

and back down the street toward the sporting goods store.

"Have you decided what we're going to get for him?" Haley asked.

"No." Maddox bit off the word. He'd been caught off guard by Danny's Christmas wish and still wasn't sure what the hell to do.

"I'm happy to help."

Haley's voice had gone soft, filling with compassion. She was beautiful when she looked like that, her cheeks flushed, eyes sparkling. Maddox still tasted her on his lips, had a vivid memory of her beneath his hands, her breasts against his chest. Heat rocked through him at the memory, not only landing in his cock but flowing around his heart.

"I told you I welcome your help," Maddox said, his words stiff. "I just don't know what we can do."

Haley's sudden smile flashed, which blasted more fire through his body. "We'll think of something. There's always *something* you can do if you put your mind to it."

Sure was. Maddox swallowed on his dry throat as Haley walked away from him. Her hips swayed, the borrowed coat brushing a fine ass in tight jeans.

*Always something you can do if you put your mind to it.*

Maddox was going to put his mind to exactly what it would take to keep Haley in Starlight Bend a little longer, as long as necessary. For what, he didn't know.

But he and Haley were poised on the edge of something, like a breath of air that was hovering, waiting, for Maddox to take it in. He wanted Haley here long enough for him to figure out what was going on and to see her smile at him like that one more time.

---

THE SPORTING GOODS STORE WAS CROWDED, THE snow not keeping people from shopping. Haley took it all in with a professional eye. The walls and counters were full of fishing gear, as she'd expected, with hunting supplies locked behind glass cases. Heads of animals unfortunate enough to be brought down with those supplies studded the walls — moose, elk, pronghorn deer.

Her attention moved to the large Christmas tree in the middle of the store, decorated with glittering ornaments and lights, surrounded by gifts. She couldn't tell whether the gifts were what people had already bought for the kids or simply wrapped empty boxes, but they gave the place a festive air.

A man in a red Santa suit was talking to a group of kids who looked to be about seven or eight. He played the part with gusto, putting his hands on his belt and saying "Ho, ho, ho," or bending down and winking to make the kids laugh.

Whoever they had playing Santa truly looked the part. He had a ruddy face, blue eyes, snowy white hair, and a beard that Haley could tell was real. He could have stepped right out of *'Twas The Night Before Christmas*.

Haley moved to Maddox. "Who is he? He's great."

Maddox shook his head. "No idea," he answered, voice brushing heat into her ear. "Never seen him before this year. Our usual Santa retired, so he must have been asked to fill in."

"Well, he knows what he's doing. Do you think I could take a gift card?"

"Don't see why not. We only have a couple of days until Christmas, though."

Santa heard them. He was gazing at Haley with an unnerving stare, as though he could read every one of her thoughts. The kids had cleared out from around him for the moment, following two women, probably teachers, who were shepherding them. Santa waved her and Maddox over with a white-gloved hand.

"Take one," he said to Haley in his deep voice. "A star on the tree means a young one in need."

He studied Haley a little longer with his piercing stare then busied himself with his red Santa sack as Haley plucked a star-shaped card from the tree. She glanced inside, smiled at what the little girl wanted, and tucked it into her pocket.

"A dollhouse," she told Maddox. "That will be fun."

She started to turn away, but Santa was suddenly in front of her. "Not so fast, young lady."

He held up his red bag, letting it fall open. "What's your hurry?"

"Oh." Haley flushed. "I wasn't hurrying—"

"She's not from around here," Maddox said, his voice light. "She likes to rush."

"I can see that." Santa gave Maddox a quelling look. "But she's our guest. And because you're a guest, you get to make a wish."

"A wish?" Haley sent Maddox a puzzled look but his expression was blank.

Santa shook his bag. "Make a wish and reach inside. See what happens."

Haley hoped there was nothing weird in there— but probably he had candy or lollipops or something like that. She closed her eyes, thought of what she was sure she wished for, and stuck her hand into the bag.

Haley came up with a simple business card between her fingers, which had red gilt around the edges and red foil writing.

*Your wish has been granted.*

# Chapter Six

꧁꧂

Haley stared at Santa, who watched her
closely.

Her wish had been granted? She'd impulsively
wished not to be trapped in this crazy town with real
Santas, huge men surrounded by fifty-year-old junk,
and hot cowboys who kissed like fire.

She looked around, but nope, she was still in the
middle of the sporting goods store in Starlight Bend,
with the hot cowboy in question hovering at her
right shoulder.

"It doesn't say *what* wish," she said, showing
Santa the card.

"Don't worry," Santa said, and winked at her.
"You'll see."

Haley opened her mouth to ask what he meant
by that, but Santa swung away, dropped his sack,
and faced the next crowd of kids being ushered in,

his hands on his belt. "Ho, ho, ho!" he bellowed, and the kids laughed.

Haley turned to Maddox, who was watching her intently. He closed his hand around her arm and led her away.

Wishing, Haley realized, was a complicated thing. She cupped the business card in her hand, the tingle in her fingers and her heart puzzling her very much.

---

AFTER A GREAT MEAL AT LAKESIDE CAFE, Maddox took them back to Andy's. Andy didn't answer when Maddox called out for him and didn't look up when Maddox towed Haley into the back to the workbench.

Haley's phone lay in about fifty pieces. Maddox heard her gasp even over the 1960s transistor radio blaring Christmas music on Andy's table.

Andy raised his head as Maddox put his fists on the bench. Andy's brown eyes were huge through the lenses of his headband magnifier, blinking at him like a goldfish through its bowl.

"Come back tomorrow," Andy said before Maddox could speak. "I'll have it done."

Andy turned away, already shutting them out of his personal space. Haley looked upset, but Maddox led her outside.

"I'll buy you a new phone," Maddox said as they

emerged and headed for the stables. "That one was probably dead anyway."

"Not the point." Haley huffed. "How am I going to make calls and order my gift?"

She pulled out the card she'd picked from the tree with the name of a girl who lived almost halfway to Kalispell. Haley had showed Maddox the card at lunch. The girl had asked for a dollhouse, a real one, where the lights worked and the windows and doors opened and closed.

"I could have one delivered," Haley said, despair in her voice. "I know a wonderful miniaturist who custom designs houses and always has readymade ones for short-notice gifts, especially at Christmas. But how am I supposed to get in touch with her?"

"Hey, now." Maddox put his hand on her shoulder, finding her quavering. It was too cold out here, hard on someone not used to it. "Everything will be okay, you'll see."

"How can you say that?" Haley's voice rang down the quiet street, to be absorbed by the thickly falling snow. "I'm stuck here, my phone's in a million pieces, I can't talk to my dad, and I'll probably miss Christmas with him. I haven't missed Christmas Eve or Christmas Day with my dad since ... well, ever."

Maddox pulled her around the other side of the empty hitching posts and put his arms around her. Haley stiffened for a moment, then slumped against him, the fight going out of her.

Something had changed. She'd been feisty and

fiery all morning, sure she'd kick the dust off this Podunk town as fast as she could.

Now she was losing hope, her resilience deflating. Maddox held on to her, wishing the strength he'd been gifted with could be transferred to her. He often wished that, watching others suffering and wanting more than anything to give them some of his toughness. If he could give one part of his strength to help someone who needed it, he would.

Maddox pulled Haley close, rubbing her back. Haley leaned her head on his chest, her wool cap tickling his chin.

She fit fine against his body, in the circle of his arms. They swayed a little together, finding warmth in each other. The street was quiet—people rarely came down this little lane except to seek out Andy.

Haley continued to shiver. She curled gloved fingers into his chest, quieting, as though she didn't mind at all standing in his embrace in a snowy side street.

When she looked up at him, Maddox brushed her lips with his, but he didn't pull her into another deep kiss. Instead he tucked a lock of hair back under her cap and released her.

"Let's get home," he said in a quiet voice. "We'll warm up and then figure out what to do."

"There's nothing *to* do," Haley said. "Except wait."

And that was killing her, he could see. Haley was a woman who ran around fixing everything in her path. Kind of like Aunt Jane, though in a different way. Maddox was figuring out that Haley thought she knew what was best for everyone and grew frustrated when she couldn't make it happen. Aunt Jane also believed she knew what was best for everyone and quietly moved heaven and earth to achieve it.

The two of them together ...

Maddox suppressed a shudder. If Haley stayed longer, he might have to move out for his own safety.

Maddox touched another kiss to her lips. He resisted the urge to kiss the hell out of her again, first because she was hurting, second because someone *would* come down this street and their encounter would provide dinner conversation for the whole town. People were already talking, Maddox knew—a kiss would put the cherry on top.

Haley looked up at him, her brown eyes full of sorrow, and broke his heart.

---

HALEY WAS VERY COLD BY THE TIME THEY reached Maddox's ranch. The house had a name, she discovered, as they rode under the arched gate—Stardust Ranch. Very poetic.

Her heart warmed in spite of her anguish when she saw the lights in the windows of the yellow house welcoming them in the early twilight. It was definitely a home.

Aunt Jane listened to Haley's tribulations

without changing expression as Maddox breezed back out to see to his horses.

Aunt Jane shrugged when Haley finished. "Everything works out for the best," she said. "If you end up here over Christmas, then it was meant to be."

"I'm meant to be with my dad in his house, cooking dinner with him," Haley said in frustration. "He needs me there."

Aunt Jane patted her hand. "There's a little bit of magic in Starlight Bend every Christmas, honey. It will be fine. You'll see. Now, you go enjoy yourself a while, and I'll call you down in time for dinner."

Haley was still full from lunch at the diner. She'd thought she'd be going light by ordering the turkey sandwich, until it had arrived — huge slabs of turkey with gravy and potatoes piled, open-faced, on home-made bread, and apple pie for dessert. Enough carbs to choke a bear. The weird thing was, no one here was obese. But if they had to walk, horseback ride, snowshoe, and ski all winter, they'd easily work off heavy meals. It wasn't a diet for people who sat at a desk all day.

Haley found books in the living room, juicy murder mysteries interspersed with books of knitting patterns. She was in the rocking chair in her bedroom, deep in a mystery when Aunt Jane announced dinner. Haley blinked, surprised she'd sat for hours absorbed in a story, no thought of going over work things on her laptop.

Aunt Jane's dinner, which Maddox returned to the house in time for, was hearty vegetable soup, thick slices of meatloaf, the inevitable potatoes — boiled this time — a salad containing winter lettuce and more veggies, and baked apples for dessert. Lance sat nearby, a hopeful look on his face. He disappeared only when Maddox dropped a chunk of meatloaf on the floor. There was a sound of slobber and a clink of tags, then Lance's head rose to peer over the table again.

"How do you all move around so fast?" Haley asked when she finished, patting her stomach. "Everyone in town zips from place to place with so much energy. I just want to go to sleep."

Maddox grinned at her. His eyes sparkled blue in the light of the candles Aunt Jane had lit around the room. For ambience, she said. The windows were dark now, flakes of snow drifting past.

"You get used to it," Maddox said. He'd put away more food than Haley and Aunt Jane together, and he looked full of life. "Horses keep you on your toes. I'm going to have to get them into the ring tomorrow. Snow is lightening up, and they've had too much time off."

"Does that mean the snowplows will be able to work?" Haley asked, but without the eagerness she'd expressed this morning. She'd already learned that Starlight Bend ran on its own schedule.

"Maybe," Aunt Jane said. "There are a lot of roads, and they plow out to people who are the worst off—ones who'd be truly stranded. We're fine here—we can get in and out to town without too much trouble."

"What about the road where my car is?"

"Who knows?" Aunt Jane said. "As long as the car's flagged, so the snowplows don't run over it."

Haley looked up in alarm, but Maddox's eyes danced. "Don't worry," he said. "Buddy took care of it. They'll see the flag before the car's a pile of fiberglass."

Haley knew he was teasing her, but she gave him a glare. "Doesn't anyone in Starlight Bend take care of anything? That's an expensive car, and my phone is now scrap. It's wasteful to be so careless."

Maddox shook his head as though she didn't understand, but Aunt Jane answered. "Of course we're not wasteful, sweetie. It's just that we value different things. A car's only good if it gets you around when you need it to. Any car or truck can do that. A phone's useful if you can't talk to someone face-to-face. But any phone will do in that case. Things can be replaced. People can't, no matter what anyone thinks."

Maddox's amusement had disappeared. Haley remembered that his parents had been killed when he'd been small—how horrible that must have been. No, people definitely couldn't be replaced. Each was unique, like her dad, and Aunt Jane, and Maddox. Lance too. Haley reached down and gave Lance's head a pat. He looked disappointed her hand didn't contain meatloaf, but he enjoyed the petting as well.

"I can't keep dogs at my apartment," Haley said wistfully. "No pets allowed."

Aunt Jane rose and began collecting dishes. "I can't imagine living like that. For people who are allergic, I can understand, but to banish all pets, period? Nope. Never living in a city if I have to do that."

Maddox winked at Haley as he started gathering dishes. Haley jumped up to help. "Inhuman," Maddox said. "Lance agrees, don't you, boy?"

Lance's tail thumped hard. Maddox grinned again and disappeared into the kitchen with his plates.

He could be such a shit. At least, he pretended to be. But he helped his aunt, looked after his animals, was kind to kids and good to his friends, like Andy, no matter how odd they were. Maddox took people as they were—didn't expect them to be anything other than themselves.

*Refreshing.*

He also kissed with hot skill and had a body to make a goddess weep. Haley stacked dishes with more energy than necessary and charged into the kitchen with them. Maddox took them from her, his strength coming through the plates she handed him.

What the hell was she going to do?

No party tonight. Maddox knew Haley was bored out of her mind, but that was life in the sticks. The television was out because of the storm, the Internet now out too.

Maddox usually went into town nights the roads were good, to hang out with friends at the bar, the town's gathering place. He didn't like to leave Aunt Jane on her own out here in the snow though, and Haley would never make another ride, especially in the cold and dark.

She was dozing while Aunt Jane knitted and Maddox caught up on newspaper reading. Lance lay on the carpet an exact distance between all three of them.

He liked this, Maddox realized. Haley warming the room with her presence, relaxing into the quiet. Maybe that's what she needed—a place to simply *stop*.

There was a lot going on inside her head, though. She was too upset at the wrong things, which meant something was bothering her more than simply being stuck at Maddox's ranch. Maddox was going to pry what she was holding in out of her. He'd learned a long time ago that hurting couldn't heal unless you ripped off the bandage.

Aunt Jane, on the dot of ten, set aside her knitting, went to the kitchen to top up Lance's food and water bowls for the night, came back out, and kissed Maddox on the cheek.

"I'm turning in," she said. "Good night, Haley."

Haley came awake. "Good night, Aunt Jane." She made no move to rise and make her way upstairs with her.

"Night, Aunt Jane," Maddox said, returning the peck on Aunt Jane's thin cheek. "Don't let the bed bugs bite."

Aunt Jane tousled his hair, as she'd done every night since he was ten, and climbed the stairs. The sound of Lance eating came through the kitchen door as Aunt Jane's footsteps faded.

"Now then, young lady," Maddox said to Haley. "You and me are going to talk."

"We are?" Haley blinked her brown-gold eyes at him. "I thought men didn't like to have heart-to-heart talks with women."

"Well, this man does. You were upset about your phone more than you were about your very expensive car being buried in a snow bank. What's up with you?"

Haley gave him a cautious look. "Nothing's *up*. I'm just unhappy that I'm snowbound, and that I can't help either myself or get the kids their gifts. That's all."

So she said, but Maddox knew there was plenty more. He wanted to know everything about Haley McKee, not just her name or her daddy's company, but about *her*. And he was running out of time. The snow would stop, Christmas would come, and his world would start again. Without Haley.

"Anyway," Haley said. "What's up with *you*?

Why does a grown man live with his aunt when you could move out your own, or leave town altogether? You have a degree in engineering, you said. You could take a job anywhere, in any city. Lots of opportunity in Seattle, where you could make a lot of money. Yet you hang out here and train horses."

"Not everything's about money," Maddox said. The words came out more harshly than he'd intended, and he closed his mouth with a snap.

"See? That's why I'm intrigued. What makes you tick, Maddox Campbell?"

Maddox held up his hand. "Tell you what. Since we're both so fired-up curious about each other, how about we make this interesting?"

Her eyes narrowed. "Interesting how?"

Maddox rose, went to the hutch where his aunt kept her best china, and rummaged in a drawer. He came out with a deck of cards.

"I told you we played checkers to while away the winter nights," he said. "I was making that up. What we really play is poker. You up to it?"

"Depends." More caution. "What do you play for?"

"Tonight, for answers. We lose a hand, we have to answer a question."

Haley was on her feet, her eyes sparkling as she answered his challenge. "And what if we really don't want to answer that question?"

"Then you have to take something off." Maddox

fixed his gaze on her, daring her to refuse. "Truth or
strip poker. Your choice."

## Chapter Seven

Haley's heart thumped but at the same time, she tasted triumph. She was good at poker, very good at it. If she could rescue a company from its death throes and bring it back piece by piece until it made billions, she could win at poker against Maddox Campbell. There was a series of careful decisions in pulling a business back from bank-ruptcy, same as in poker.

Haley would pry all this man's secrets from him and maybe have a look at his nice body too. They both wore layers of clothes against the cold, but all those layers wouldn't help him in the long run.

"What about Aunt Jane?" Haley asked, glancing up the stairs. "I don't think she'll approve."

"Aunt Jane sleeps hard," Maddox said. He ran his thumb over the edges of the cards, snapping them together. "We can do this in my room if you want more privacy."

"*My* room," Haley said quickly. "You're a bachelor. I'm sure mine's neater."

"Huh. You never grew up with Aunt Jane." Maddox slapped the cards to his other hand. "But okay."

He started up the stairs, not waiting for her. Lance woke up, snorted, and followed.

Haley scrambled to her feet, jogging to keep up with them both. Maddox walked calmly down the hall and into her room, which overlooked the front yard. Aunt Jane's bedroom was in the back, Maddox's and another spare room in between hers and Haleys'.

Lance hurried in, tail moving. Haley didn't object—if they shut Lance out, he'd only scratch and whine until they let him in. Maddox shut the door all but a crack behind them, so Lance could paw his way out when he wished.

Maddox dragged the chair from the desk and turned it around to face the bed. He sat down, divided the deck in two, and began to shuffle the cards expertly on the bedspread.

Haley climbed onto the bed, sitting with her back to the headboard. She started to slide off her shoes, then thought better of it. Better to leave as many items on as possible.

Maddox continued to shuffle. "Five-card stud? Or Texas Hold-'Em?"

"Five-card is faster," Haley said. "And more risky."

"All right." Maddox's blue eyes glinted as though she'd sealed her fate. He dealt out the cards then slapped the pack facedown on the bedspread. Lance sank to the floor with a huff of breath and lowered his head to the carpet.

They didn't bother with the usual betting rules or wild cards. What they had at the end of each hand would decide who won.

The first deal gave Haley a lousy pair of twos. She ditched the other three cards, took the replacements Maddox dealt her, and ended up with an ace to go with her twos, but nothing more.

"Call," Maddox said, watching her carefully.

Haley sighed and laid down her cards. Her heart beat faster until Maddox dropped his hand. He had five unmatched cards, nothing at all.

Haley grinned in victory. "Ha. Okay, first question," she said as Maddox gathered the cards and stacked them together. "Why is a handsome cowboy like you not married? You take too long in the shower in the mornings? Do you criticize your girl-friends' cooking? What? Either answer or lose a garment."

Maddox scowled. He pressed his lips together, reached down, drew off one boot, and dropped it to the floor with a *clunk*.

He lifted the cards and held them out to Haley. "Your deal," he growled.

Haley only smiled at him. This would be more fun than she'd thought.

She dealt herself a pair of queens. She laid them down with gusto at the end of the hand, then gave a groan of dismay when Maddox dropped a pair of jacks and a pair of kings on top of them.

"My question," Maddox said without pausing to gloat. "You were upset when you saw what Danny's wish was. I mean, really angry, like it was personal. Why?" He leaned a little toward her, his blue eyes dark in the bedroom's weak light.

Haley considered the question then slid off one shoe, showed it to him, and dropped it to the floor.

Maddox only picked up the cards in silence. He won the next hand as well with three of a kind. "Same question," he said.

For answer, Haley dropped another shoe. Lance raised his head and studied it, then lowered his chin back down, his eyes drifting closed.

"All right," Maddox said warningly. "If you want to play it that way."

Half an hour later, Haley had lost her sweater and both stockings, and now sat in her slacks and the tank top she'd worn under the sweater. Maddox had only his jeans and a white tank, his sweatshirt, belt, and socks on the floor. His muscles stretched the tank, curls of dark hair showing at the neckline.

"*Now* it will get interesting," Haley said, shuffling the cards for her deal.

Maddox lost to Haley's four of a kind. Before she could ask her question, he growled and pulled the tank top off over his head.

A finely honed chest came into view, along with tight abs, his pecs dusted with very black hair. Haley ran an appreciative gaze over him, not pretending not to look.

"Don't get too cold like that," she said, handing him the deck.

"The heater works," Maddox said. "Get ready to answer some questions, sweetheart."

Haley picked up the five cards he tossed out, then hid her disquiet when she had nothing that matched—but she did have the ace of hearts. She dumped four cards, keeping the ace and at least picked up a couple more hearts. Nothing that would make a flush, a straight, or even a pair, damn it.

"Tell you what," Maddox said. "I only have two pieces of clothing left. I'm guessing you have four. I'm willing to stake all I have on this hand. Are you?"

He was bluffing—he must be. He wanted to get her naked, or at least make her desperate enough to tell him her life story.

Then again, he might be sitting on a royal or straight flush. The odds of those were low, Haley knew. That's why they beat everything else.

Hell, even a pair would win over what Haley had right now. Her only safety was the ace—if Maddox had nothing, she would at least win the hand.

"My counteroffer," she said, studying her cards calmly, as though *she* had a royal flush. "I'll give you two to one. My shirt and pants for your jeans. And hope we don't freeze."

"I told you, it's plenty warm in here. You're just not used to actual winter. But okay. I'll take you up on that."

"Good," Haley said lightly. "I call."

Maddox's eyes sparkled in sudden mirth. "Full house."

"Shit," Haley said, her heart banging. She threw her cards down on top of his pair of tens and triple eights.

"You don't have to strip off," Maddox said. "You can talk to me instead."

Haley gave him a cool look. They'd drawn closer together as they'd played, Maddox leaning over the bed, Haley more in the middle, no longer against the headboard. She sat cross-legged, the cards near her bare feet. Maddox rested his elbows on the bed, his head close enough that she could stroke his hair if she wanted to. Beyond them, Lance stretched across the carpet, snoring.

Haley no longer felt tight and restricted. Maybe because she'd lost some binding clothes, maybe because tension had lessened between her and Maddox. Games and undressing could do that.

She could tell him about her mom ditching her dad when Haley was little, running off with the photographer Dad had hired to do their portraits. Haley had been furious with her mother for years—

still was. Dad had gone to pieces, and Haley had been only ten.

She could explain all this to Maddox, knowing Maddox would understand. People who'd lost their parents young did.

But Haley played to win. She'd have Maddox Campbell out of his clothes, and feast her eyes on him or find out what secrets nestled in his heart. She wouldn't admit defeat until it was actually defeat. No giving up too soon.

She uncrossed her legs and rolled off the bed to her feet. Facing Maddox, no wilting, Haley unbuttoned and unzipped her pants, letting them fall in a puddle around her ankles. She stepped out of them then grasped the hem of her tank top and pulled it off over her head.

Maddox looked at her without embarrassment. He didn't ogle or leer but calmly ran his gaze from her green lacy bra cupping her breasts to the matching silk panties on her hips.

"Very Christmassy," he said.

Haley shrugged. "I have a red pair for the day. Not with me, though. I assumed I'd be home." She swallowed the catch in her throat.

"Those will work." Maddox gathered the cards and started shuffling. It was Haley's deal, but Maddox seemed to have forgotten that. "I guess the next hand will decide it."

"If we both go all in, sure."

Maddox kept shuffling, watching Haley climb

back onto the bed and sit down in her place. The bedspread held a warm indent where she'd been, which felt good. Maddox was right that she wasn't used to winter cold, but she refused to shiver and reach for a blanket. Seattle certainly could be chilly and dank but didn't hold the bone-penetrating cold of the Montana mountains.

Maddox's blunt fingers skillfully shuffled the cards, arching them up to fall gracefully back into the pack.

He dealt, his eyes flicking to her bare knee and then back to the cards. Maddox picked up his hand, scanning it. His eyebrows went up. "Hmm. Interesting."

"Okay, now I know you're bluffing," Haley said. "You never look at your hand and use words like *interesting* in front of the other players."

Maddox sent her a cryptic look. "I'm just saying it's interesting."

Lance rose to his feet, stretched, and shook himself. He sauntered to the door, pawed it open, then slunk out. Maddox got off the bed and closed the door all the way behind him. "I don't think we need an audience for this last part."

"He'll try to get back in," Haley pointed out.

"Nah, he'll go sleep on my bed. Now let's play."

Haley hugged her cards to her chest as Maddox came back around the bed to his place. "No looking at my hand," she said.

"Sugar, it's not your *hand* I'm looking at."

Haley flushed as Maddox resumed his seat, resting his arms on his knees, his bare feet on the bed's rail.

She scanned her cards, which weren't bad—three tens—and tossed away a card. "One, please," she said.

Maddox touched the deck. "Just one? Are you sure?"

"I'm sure. May I have the card?"

Maddox slid it to her. Haley took it, forcing herself not to change expression. "Thank you," she said calmly.

"Dealer takes three."

Haley glanced at him. Perspiration beaded on his temples. "I thought you said your hand was interesting," she said.

"It is. But I want three cards." He drew them without a tremor, though the perspiration at his temples deepened.

"Are you ready to call?" Haley asked.

"All or nothing," Maddox reminded her. "Are you sure?"

"I'm quite sure."

"Now I know you have a decent hand." Maddox gave her a shrewd look. "You have a tell."

Haley peered at him. "I do *not* have a tell. What are you talking about?"

"Whenever you have good cards, you're more polite. Like you can afford to be condescending."

Haley met his gaze with a lofty one. "Is that so?"

"That's so. Ready to show me all you've got?"

"You wish." Haley laid down her cards with a flourish. "Full house. Tens and queens. Lose the clothes, Campbell. Or talk." Her heart beat faster. She hoped he'd choose to strip—there had to be some fine man under those jeans.

"Not so fast, sweetheart." Maddox's frown turned into a broad smile. "Straight flush. As they say—read 'em and weep."

*"Damn."* Haley's mouth popped open. The cards stared up at her, the six, seven, eight, nine, and ten of hearts. "How did you get a straight flush?"

"I kept two hearts and drew three more. I guess it's my lucky night."

"Wait—you got up to let Lance out. You had cards hidden by the door, right?"

Maddox sat back in his chair, propping his feet on the bed. "Oh, so now you're accusing me of cheating? Sore loser. I drew those cards fair as anything."

Haley knew he had. Maddox probably prided himself on being painfully honest. "Shit," she whispered.

Her palms had gone slick, her breath tight in her chest. But of course, she didn't have to take off her underwear—she could tell him her life's story instead. Or simply rise to her feet with as much dignity as she could in a bright green bra and panties and demand that he leave. Or, she could finish the game like a good sport and take them off.

Why did baring her entire body to him seem less intimidating than exposing her heart?

She slid a shaking hand behind her, resting her fingers on the bra's hooks. "If I do this, you have to join in. I'm not a stripper putting on a show."

Maddox's chest rose. "Nice idea. You doing a pole dance."

Haley's face heated, but she refused to let him discomfit her. "Ha. I'd fall on my face. Pole dancing is hard—athletic even. Strippers aren't given enough respect."

"Tell you what—if I ever find myself at a club, I'll give them lots of respect." Maddox put his hand to his waistband. "But sure. I'll join you."

He unbuttoned his jeans. In the silence of the room, the sound of his zipper was loud.

Haley's breath nearly choked her. It filled her lungs too quickly, the air and light in the room swirling together in sparkling colors. She unhooked her bra, the band loosening.

Maddox slid out of his jeans, revealing a pair of tight black boxer-briefs. Didn't help Haley catch her breath.

He put his strong knee on the bed. "How about I make this easier on both of us?"

Maddox slid one arm around Haley's back. His hand went to the loose bra strap, pushing it open, his palm a place of incredible warmth.

Their gazes locked as Maddox guided Haley up to him. She closed the space between them quickly, lifting herself against him and offering her mouth in a long, hungry kiss.

## Chapter Eight

※

Warm arms enclosed him, warm legs too. Haley pulled Maddox down to her, her lips seeking his, her body wrapping around him.

Maddox laid her down, bracing himself on his knees as he lowered to her. They lost the kiss and Haley looked up at him, her brown eyes full of tenderness but also consternation.

She didn't like letting herself go, his corporate lady. He'd watched her hang back and assess every situation before tentatively wading forward. Unlike Maddox, who'd learned to jump on in, to hell with it.

Maddox kissed the bridge of her nose. He freed her from the bra and tossed it off the bed, then ran his fingers down the curve of her breast.

"I knew you were beautiful," he said, moving his kiss to her cheekbone. "I knew it the minute I looked into your car window, and you screamed bloody murder."

"You scared me." Haley turned her head, catching his lips in a soft kiss. "I was alone, stranded."

"You never have to be alone, sweetheart." Maddox kissed the curve of her lower lip, her chin, her cheek. "Doesn't matter if we go our separate ways. I'll be there for you, whenever you need me."

She stared up at him in surprise, but Maddox made no empty promise. All Haley had to do was pick up the phone, and he'd go to her, no questions asked.

Haley said softly, "When I stopped being scared, I thought I'd never seen eyes as blue as yours."

"No, when you stopped being scared, you were mad as hell." Maddox smiled into her cheek. "And you kept on being beautiful."

"Shut up and kiss me," Haley whispered.

Maddox complied. He parted her lips, swept his tongue into her mouth, tasted her fire. Haley ran her foot up his bare leg, her breasts soft cushions for his chest.

Both of them knew what would happen—what was happening. Haley's fingers moved through his hair then down to his back. She was strong and yet softness itself.

Maddox lifted away from her warmth, not wanting to, but he had to before it was too late. He was hard, his underwear constricting, but he'd have to make himself wait a few moments longer.

He touched the tip of her nose. "Do *not* go away."

Haley raised her head as Maddox leapt from the bed and made for the door. He pulled it open silently, not waking the sleeping house, and dashed to his own bedroom.

He moved fast, not wanting to give Haley time to close her door and lock him out. Maddox noted distractedly as he grabbed what he needed from his top dresser drawer, that Lance had curled up in the middle of his bed.

"Good dog," he whispered, then ran back out again.

He'd been gone maybe twenty seconds. He closed and locked Haley's door and half fell back on the bed.

Maddox offered no explanation for the foil-wrapped condom he tossed to her night table, only came back down to Haley. The condom was just in case. They might decide, like two rational adults, not to make love at all.

Sure. No way in hell were they going to be rational. It was almost Christmas and they were two lonely people together in this quiet house, crystal snow falling against the window.

Some kind of Christmas magic had brought them together. Maddox was going to enjoy it instead of fighting it. From the look in Haley's brown-gold eyes, she'd decided that too.

He could also tell from the way she hooked her

fingers around his underwear and pulled it down that she was more than ready. Her touch went to his ass as their kisses deepened, her small hands cupping it.

Maddox shoved his underwear the rest of the way off. As much as he liked her fondling his backside, he made himself slide away from her. He backed off the bed then reached down and pulled the Christmas-green undies from Haley's hips.

As the silken underwear joined his utilitarian boxer-briefs on the rug, Maddox dragged in a breath and looked down at Haley.

*Damn.* She lay back on her elbows, her tawny hair falling across her cheeks, her eyes languid. Her body was on display for him, the position pushing her toward him a little. Her strong shoulders led to the softest curve of breasts, her nipples dark pink, the tips tight.

Her stomach was probably less firm than she liked—women thought they had to have some strange hourglass shape—her hips wide and lush. Her legs were strong like her shoulders, with muscles of a woman who enjoyed walking and running. Between her thighs, a swirl of golden hair beckoned his touch.

Maddox's cock was harder than he ever remembered it being, his hunger for her escalating to fever levels. He'd craved her since he'd pulled her from her car, when she'd slipped and he'd caught her against him.

*Made for me.* The words had whispered through his mind.

Haley's smile was sultry. "You're hot, cowboy."

Maddox flushed. "Yeah, I'm burning up."

She laughed, inhibitions flowing away. "Come and warm me."

Maddox held himself back from leaping directly on top of her. Maybe one day, when they were more comfortable with each other, they could play, but right now, he only wanted to be with her.

He lowered himself to the bed, aching with impatience, and stretched his body over hers. Her wrists ended up in his big hands, held gently against the mattress.

"You are the best thing I ever did see," Maddox said, his voice becoming thick. "Worth digging out of that snow bank."

She only smiled, loosened her hand from his hold, and touched his face.

The touch was feather light and so tender that what was left of Maddox's control dissolved. He had enough self-command to drag the condom from the nightstand, rip it open, and quickly push it over his cock. Haley helped him, her shaking fingers driving him wild.

Maddox lowered her to the bed and slid his hand between her legs. She was already plenty warm, as ready for this as he was. Maddox drew a breath and slid himself inside her.

*Hot, tight, sweet.* The exhilarating feelings

streamed through him, his eyes closing as he fought a groan. Haley made a noise in her throat and touched his face again with smooth fingertips. Then her hands returned to his backside to pull him all the way in.

Maddox paused, buried inside her, the two of them joined. He looked into her eyes, and found warmth, beauty, and the amazing heart of this woman.

Haley gazed up at him in return, the look on her face enough to melt him.

Staying still any longer wasn't an option. Maddox withdrew halfway and came back to her in a hard thrust. Haley's eyes heated, her smile widening as she lifted her hips to meet his.

He thrust again, and she rocked against him, the two of them establishing a rhythm without speaking. Excitement escalated through Maddox, making thought waver and feeling take over.

The quiet of the night, broken by the occasional flurry of snow slapping the window like grains of sand heightened the intensity—no noise, only Haley and Maddox alone in the dark, glittering world.

Haley sank her fingers into his hips, urging him faster. Maddox stifled the sounds he wanted to make, knowing his aunt and his dog slept not far down the hall. This had to be silent loving.

Haley's body heated, her limbs becoming loose, her kisses fervent. As Maddox thrust harder, the bed creaking, she lolled her head back in release, a cry escaping her mouth.

Maddox caught the sound on his lips, kissing her as he rode her, thrusting faster and faster. He wanted to go on forever, but his world squeezed suddenly to one single point of awareness.

*Haley.*

"Damn it," he said in a fierce whisper, then he kissed her again, riding it out.

When Maddox could think once more, he found himself holding her, kissing her lips in wonderful afterglow. Haley held on to him, her mouth hot, her body welcoming.

They sank into the bedding, Maddox clumsily reaching for a blanket to pull over them as they snuggled down. The world went still, snow whispering at the window. Haley touched his lips, bathing him in the best smile he'd ever seen.

WHEN HALEY AWOKE THE FIRST TIME IN THE night, Maddox was with her, his legs around hers, the two of them tucked into the small bed. He'd rid himself of the condom a while back, but they'd had plenty of fun with hands and kisses bringing each other to enjoyment. Now they basked in warmth and sleep. Haley smiled in contentment and drifted off again.

The next time she woke, she found Maddox gone and the window just beginning to lighten.

She stared at a blank sky, gray with clouds. The view should have been gloomy, but in the lingering memory of Maddox's body on hers, his gentle touches, his strength when he loved her, the sky might have been brilliant blue with rainbows dancing through it.

Maddox's lovemaking had been an astonishing mix of passion and generosity, he enjoying it yet giving her as much pleasure as he could. Haley basked for a while thinking about it, then she sat up abruptly.

They'd hit the solstice, which meant days were at their shortest. If it was already light outside, she'd overslept by a long way.

Haley tore the covers from her naked body, sprang out of bed, and tripped over the large body of Lance. Catching herself in time, she stumbled to her suitcase, yanked out her last set of clean clothes and hopped awkwardly trying to put them on. Not easy with a giant dog taking up most of the room.

Haley stuffed her arms into a thick pullover sweater, dragged on her shoes, and hurried from the room. She smelled the lingering odors of coffee and bacon as she plunged down the stairs, followed noisily by Lance.

It was nine-thirty by the clock on the landing. Haley jogged into the kitchen to find Aunt Jane washing dishes, a plate of food resting on the stove.

"I kept it warm for you," Aunt Jane said without turning around.

"Sorry." Haley took up the plate and carried it to the table. Lance was already sitting by her chair. "I should have set an alarm. I didn't mean to oversleep."

"Mmm." Aunt Jane glanced over her shoulder. The look in her eyes made Haley's face scald.

Aunt Jane wasn't judgmental or disapproving. But her expression told Haley that she knew exactly what her nephew and Haley had been doing in her bedroom last night—that they were fools for thinking they could keep it a secret.

Haley ducked her head and started eating breakfast.

"Maddox almost got married," Aunt Jane said as though continuing a conversation begun some time ago. She shut off the water and started wiping the counters. "When he came back from college. He'd met a girl in California—fell madly in love. She was happy to be with him, until he brought her here and told her he wanted to live at the ranch." Aunt Jane shook her head. "I'd never heard so much arguing. She wanted him to move with her to Los Angeles and find a job. She wanted restaurants and clubs and a big house with a pool. Can't blame her really—it's what she understood, and small-town life isn't for everyone. Maddox was thinking about compromising—maybe a smaller city in California or Oregon, closer to Starlight Bend—but she walked out. He'd bought the ring and everything. She said he was a hopeless, shit-kicking cowboy in a dirty little town, and she'd never marry someone who smelled like crap. Maddox was furious, said good riddance. But I could see that it broke his heart."

Haley listened, indignation warring with compassion for Maddox. "What a bitch," she declared. She fed a piece of bacon to Lance. "Maybe small-town life *isn't* for everyone, but there's nothing wrong with *Maddox*. And Starlight Bend is beautiful. Who couldn't think so?"

"They were young," Aunt Jane said. "Hard to compromise when you're twenty-two and don't know how short life really is."

Aunt Jane turned away to continue cleaning, and Haley attacked her eggs and bacon in silence. Here was her answer as to why Maddox had never married.

Maybe the woman leaving him had made him gun-shy. No wonder Maddox had given Haley such shit—she was a big-city girl and hadn't been very complimentary about being stuck in this corner of Montana. He must have thought her just like his ex.

"He never proposed to anyone else?" Haley asked as she took her last bite. She carried her plate to the sink and rinsed it off. "That was a while ago."

"Seven years. Maddox is twenty-nine. No, the girls he grew up with are either married or gone— mostly both. Starlight Bend has a smaller proportion of women to men, and he hasn't ventured outside it to look elsewhere. High time he did, I'm thinking."

Aunt Jane squarely met Haley's gaze. Haley regarded her kind but no-nonsense face and said, "I have no intention of hurting him."

Aunt Jane shrugged. "Might be too late for that." She glanced out the window and jerked her chin. "He's coming now. Don't tell him I told you."

Maddox was swinging down from Sammy. He tossed the reins to Buddy and made for the back porch.

Haley didn't have time to give Aunt Jane more than a reassuring nod, because Maddox headed into the kitchen with a determined stride.

"Got your phone back." He held it up. "Works just fine now. I told you Andy can fix anything."

## Chapter Nine

"Dad!" Haley sang out his name as he answered the phone. She was alone in the living room, Aunt Jane keeping to the kitchen and Maddox out doing what he did with horses. Lance had followed Maddox, so Haley sat by herself.

"Hey there, pumpkin." Her dad sounded relieved but as though trying to be nonchalant. "How's the winter wonderland?"

"Very pretty—but *cold*. If I'd have known, I would have packed long underwear."

"So long as you're all right." He didn't mask the relief this time. "I was a little worried."

No, he'd been a lot worried, Haley could tell. "I'm so sorry. My phone wouldn't work—nothing would. I'm a long way from a town bigger than a postage stamp, and my car's kind of buried."

"It's all right, sweetheart. Linda told me she got

your texts, so I knew you were okay. Where are you exactly?"

"Little place called Starlight Bend, in Montana. It's beautiful. Great spot for a summer vacation."

Her father burst out laughing, his worry abating. "Vacation? Haley, you haven't taken vacation in ten years. You wouldn't know what to do on vacation."

"I'd go hiking and fishing," Haley answered. "So I hear."

Dad continued to laugh. "I'm just glad you're safe and sound."

"I'm not sure when they'll have my car free. There's only one guy in town with a plow—if the roads aren't clear by Christmas, apparently, he doesn't work that day. But I'm going to try very hard to be home for Christmas Eve dinner, Dad. I promise—"

"Slow down, pumpkin." His endearments warmed her—he was the only one who could use them without irritating Haley. Except Aunt Jane now. And, all right, Maddox. "If you can't make it, you can't. We can open presents and have dinner any day after you get back. Frankly, honey, I'm kind of glad you're stuck there. You need a little time away from the office."

"Not *this* much time. The whole Chicago deal will probably dry up because I haven't gotten the contracts started ..."

"*I* have the contracts started. I do know a thing or two about our business, you know, sweetheart. I want you to relax and not stress over anything. You just enjoy a downhome, old-fashioned Christmas. What's this I hear about a handsome cowboy?"

*Linda* ... Haley hid a growl. "I was joking. Maddox—that's his name—he dug me out of the car, and I'm staying at his place. I mean, his aunt's place. His aunt lives here too. I'm not having a dirty weekend."

Her face flamed even as she spoke. Last night, Maddox had been warm in the dark, his hands and mouth all over her, lovemaking like she'd never experienced in her life.

Not that she had the chance for much in her busy days, and she was always careful about who got close to her. But Maddox won the prize for the man who'd made her feel the most sexy, most cared for, wanted for *herself*.

"Well, maybe you should have a dirty weekend," her father shocked her by saying. "You work far too much, Haley. It's time you thought about your own life."

"My own life?" Haley repeated in bewilderment. "I'm CEO of our company. That *is* my life."

"You listen to me, pumpkin." Dad's voice went stern, barely softened by the pet name. "There's much more to life than accounts and deals. That's fine for the office, but you have to live beyond that. Take it from me. I didn't pay attention to my personal life until it was far too late—I assumed it would still be there when I was ready for it. Well, it wasn't. You have to hang on to people you care about as hard as you can, because one day you turn around, and they're gone."

His voice held sadness and finality. Haley's mother had certainly vanished abruptly—there one morning, gone by that night. She'd left a note explaining what she'd done but never came back.

"That's why I don't go very far from you, Dad," Haley said quietly. "I don't want you to find me gone too."

Her father was silent a moment. When he spoke again, he was less abrupt. "I know, sweetie. But I'm all right now, you know that. I want to see you with someone who makes you happy—for *you*, not because of the business. If it's this cowboy, well then, he has my blessing. I like horses."

Haley gave a nervous laugh. "It's nothing like that. Maddox doesn't— He isn't— I don't think this is going anywhere."

"From the sound of your voice, I'm guessing it could go somewhere. I'd like to meet him. Maybe I'll come out for your snowed-in Christmas."

"You can't," Haley said quickly. "I mean, the roads are piled high, and even if the nearest airport reopens ..."

She couldn't say why she didn't want her father coming to Montana. Not right now. Starlight Bend seemed to be frozen in a bubble—like a snow scene in glass—forever perfect. If she let her real life in, the globe would shatter, leaving only ruined remains.

Her father's voice filled with amusement. "I understand. Why don't you talk to your cowboy, and if he's willing, he can come up to Seattle. He should know what he's getting into."

"He'd never come to Seattle," Haley said with conviction. "Maddox made it clear he likes to stay home."

He'd chosen Starlight Bend over following his fiancé to Los Angeles, where he could find a job that paid him well. He'd chosen the wide-open spaces over the city's polluted sky and wall-to-wall traffic.

"If he's serious about you, he'll come," her father said, quietly confident. "It's time for you to choose your path, Haley. Right now, leave the work to me and don't worry about anything until after Christmas. Try to enjoy your accidental vacation."

Haley was already enjoying it, if she admitted it. "I love you, Dad."

"Love you too, pumpkin. I'll let everyone here know you're fine. Bye-bye, sweetheart."

"Oh, Dad, wait …"

Haley's mind flooded with all the other things she wanted to accomplish—buying the dollhouse, getting something for Danny. "There's a couple things I'm going to need your help with."

---

IT WAS STILL TOO SNOWY AND COLD TO TRAIN, BUT Buddy and Maddox took the horses around the covered ring to exercise them. Horses that stood around in their stalls became stale and cranky. Not good for them or for Maddox.

Riding also gave Maddox an excuse to stay away from Haley. She'd grabbed her phone in wild delight then disappeared into the living room, where she apparently was still talking. Maddox could see her through the window whenever he looked toward the house, phone glued to her ear.

She'd be making arrangements to haul ass out of there. Maddox imagined a helicopter cutting through the clouds, scattering snow, and Haley running joyfully to it. She'd rise into the sky and be gone, out of his life forever.

Last night had been amazing. Haley was a wonderful lover, there every moment, her kisses and touches full of fire. No faking it. She'd given all she was, and Maddox had enjoyed bringing her to pleasure again and again. If he could look forward to Haley every day, things would be perfect.

She'd be unhappy stuck in Starlight Bend, though. Haley was restless, while Starlight Bend was a study in the slow life.

Not that Maddox could describe his existence as *slow*. There was always something to do with the horses, visits to his cousins in Austin—or they came up here to choose which horses they wanted. The house was lively with one or more of the Campbell brothers around—Grant and Tyler with their clowning, Adam who could be all business but relaxing enough to talk and laugh, Carter who was efficient in his quiet way.

In the summer, Maddox taught kids to take care of horses, and he did shows and rodeos. In between he'd take Aunt Jane to Kalispell, or Missoula, or even Spokane to shop and do whatever she needed. On rare occasions, Maddox was able to sit down and enjoy a little quiet fishing, but working with horses wasn't exactly an easy life.

Haley didn't know much about horses though. She liked buildings, offices, fluorescent lights, computers ... indoor stuff. She thought Starlight Bend and the country was pretty, but how soon would that pall?

Then again, how long could Maddox live in a city, inside all the time, no place to just *walk*. Out here, he could stride for miles with nothing to hem him in. He'd die in a city. But would Haley fare any better in the country?

And why was he trying hard to figure out how not to let her go? Why was he so determined to find a way, to have a chance?

Because she was Haley. Beautiful, take-no-shit, able to stand toe-to-toe with him, but with flashes of gentleness. She truly cared about the kids and the gift tree, got along terrific with Aunt Jane, and liked dogs. No, *ew, get that slobbering, hairy thing away from me.* Haley talked to Lance as though he understood her—and he did—let him sleep with her, dropped him tidbits from the table. She'd been timid with

Sammy at first, but was now coming around to like him too.

Would she be that accepting of Maddox?

He tried to put his spinning thoughts aside while he and Buddy worked with the horses, but it was difficult. Buddy watched him narrowly, as though wondering what had him so distracted. When Buddy caught Maddox watching the house, his narrow look turned to a knowing grin. Maddox sent him a scowl, which made Buddy only grin harder.

By the time Maddox sent Buddy home for lunch and walked back to the house, Haley was still on the phone.

She breezed into the kitchen, saying good-bye to her friend Linda, then finally took the phone from her ear and beamed a huge smile at Maddox and Aunt Jane. Maddox had thought her pretty when she was furious—she was even more beautiful when happy.

"Talked to my dad and to my friend who makes the dollhouses," Haley was saying. "Dad will send a dollhouse with a friend in a private plane so it will get here by Christmas morning. My dad said he'll scour the stores for a remote-control plane for Danny. Is that all right with you, Maddox? If you'd rather get him something else, I can tell him. Oh, and even better." Her smile was huge. "I found Danny's dad."

MADDOX STARED AT HER WITHOUT BLINKING AS she spoke, then as Haley announced that she'd located Danny's father, Pete Vining, which hadn't been all that difficult, Maddox barreled to her, took her by the shoulder, and pushed her into the living room.

"What the hell do you mean, you found Danny's dad?"

Maddox's fingers bit down, and his blue eyes held nothing of the warmth they'd had when he'd loved her last night. Even during the poker game, his eyes had sparkled with good humor and wickedness. Now he was angry.

Haley jerked from his grip. "I mean, my dad found him for us. He's in a prison in eastern Oregon."

"I know that," Maddox said in a hard voice.

Haley blinked. "You know? Shit, Maddox, why didn't you say so? My dad and his assistant spent all morning calling all over the place, tracking him down. How do *you* know?"

"I asked around, and asked Buddy to ask around. Can't keep much secret in this town. Turns out Danny's mom knows exactly where her husband —now her ex-husband—is, and is happy he's there. Pete was a bad man, Haley."

"I realize that. But my dad was able to speak to him—his lawyer got him through. Danny's dad sounded so happy to hear about his son and wants to see him."

"That's not for you do decide," Maddox returned. "It's for Danny's mom to agree to, and for his lawyers and hers, and the wardens and social workers. You can't know on the basis of a phone call whether he's safe for Danny to visit."

"I *know*." Haley huffed a breath. "I'm not a complete idiot. But at least we can give Danny the choice. If it's a matter of cost to get him there ..."

Maddox's look turned fierce. "Not everything can be solved with money, sugar. Maybe you can buy anything you want, including a fancy-ass car because you need a ride across seven states, but that doesn't mean you can tell people what to do with their lives. I'll buy Danny a new fishing rod and take him out on the ice—*I'll* do things with him a dad would do. Keep your expensive presents to yourself."

Haley stared at him in hurt surprise a moment, then her anger returned. She stepped up to him, looking him straight in the eye. "Money isn't something I throw around or take for granted, Maddox Campbell. It's a tool—sometimes you use it to solve problems like trying to get yourself home in time for Christmas. Sometimes you make kids happy with it by giving them great presents. Sometimes you help a kid reunite with his dad—*if* he and his mom want him to."

She drew a ragged breath, waiting for Maddox to yell at her. When he didn't, she rushed on. "I *know* money can't solve every problem. Do you think that if money could have brought my mother back, I would have done everything in my power to make it happen? My mom didn't care at all about money—she wanted romance and attention, and my dad was too busy to give it to her. Too busy working hard so we could eat—the business was going down the toilet. He wouldn't tell us, just worked his fingers to the bone trying to keep us going. But that wasn't good enough for my mom. She hightailed it out of there when something more exciting came along." Tears stung Haley's eyes. "*That* is why I was so angry when I saw Danny's Christmas wish. Because I know exactly how he feels. Because I wrote letters to Santa for years asking him to bring my mother back to me."

Maddox stood very still. His scowl had faded as Haley had babbled, but now she couldn't see his face through the blur of tears.

"Haley." He was against her, his warm hands on her shoulders.

Haley leaned to him before she could stop herself. Maddox was large, strong, real. Nothing else seemed to be right now.

He stroked her hair, his lips pressing the top of her head. He smelled of the outdoors, country wind, cold, fresh air. Scents she had little experience with, and now they nestled in her heart.

"I lost my folks when I was a kid," he said softly. "But I never wrote letters to Santa asking for them. I knew it wouldn't do any good."

Haley gazed up at him, her chest tight. She'd at least had hope that her mom would change her mind, contact her, or come home. Maddox had known the grim truth, had learned about loss and grief far too young.

"I guess we're a couple of sad cases," she said.

"Nothing funny about it." Maddox pulled her close, a hot kiss touching her temple. "Kids shouldn't have to go through that. Danny shouldn't." He kissed her again. "It was good of you to try to help him."

"I planned to speak to his mom first," Haley said. She wiped her eyes with the back of her hand. "My dad didn't promise Danny's dad anything. I know a lot has to be taken into consideration. But my dad said the man did seem remorseful, wanting his family."

"We'll see," Maddox conceded cautiously. "It's nothing we need to fight about, sweetheart."

Haley nodded. She didn't want to fight with Maddox. Not right now. Verbal sparring with him was a lot of fun, but her prior life was edging back in. "The friends flying in the toys offered to take me home on the plane," she said. "But I'd rather drive my car. So I guess you're stuck with me a few more days."

"Not necessarily."

Haley pulled back and looked at him. She'd already made the decision—though she hadn't quite admitted it to herself—that her father was right, and she needed some time away from work. Time to do nothing, to be with people, to see if what she'd started with Maddox would go anywhere.

"What are you talking about?" she asked.

"Buddy and a couple of guys said they'd help dig out your car, now that the snow's slowed. Roads around town are still blocked, but they might be able to get you to a highway that's been cleared. Tow you if necessary. Then you can be on your way. Once you get down to the 90, you'll be fine. Home in time for Christmas."

## Chapter Ten

"Oh."

Haley didn't look happy. Which made no sense. If Maddox had told her two days ago that he could dig out her car, she'd have been rushing out the door.

A wisp of hair fell into her eyes as she stared at him, and Haley brushed it impatiently away. "It's kind of you."

"Thank Buddy. He's resourceful. Has to be, living in the hollow he does. He's became a genius at getting out of the snow."

Haley rubbed her arms. "I see. Well." She wet her lips. "I guess I'd better go pack."

"It'll be a while," Maddox warned. "I'm heading out to help them."

"Great. Thanks."

Aunt Jane banged in from the kitchen, followed by Lance. "Are you done yelling at each other now?"

She looked from one to the other. "Good. Haley, I'll help you pack. But consider staying on through Christmas, all right? We'd love to have you."

Haley rubbed her arms again. "If I can make it home, I should try. I hate to think of my dad alone."

Aunt Jane nodded, not offended. "I understand, honey. Let's go sort you out. You'll want to wash those clothes first, so you have something clean to wear on the road."

---

HALEY'S CAR LOOKED SMALL AND PATHETIC HALF buried in snow, surrounded by Buddy and his friends with shovels. The guys had cleared a path to it and were now digging down to the wheels, banging shovels and picks into the frozen crust to loosen it.

Haley had loved the sleek car when she'd seen it in the showroom, but now it looked tiny and forlorn, a frivolous whim of the moment. The giant pickups surrounding the car were much more practical for this terrain and weather.

Maddox had brought her on Sammy, riding with his arms around her, as he had when he'd rescued her. The plan was to free the car, get it back to the ranch, and then help her make her way west to the main highway. The road from Maddox's ranch house to the highway was packed with snow but at least drivable — or so Maddox said.

Buddy kicked the last of the snow from the front tires as Maddox helped Haley down from Sammy's back. "Start it up," Buddy called to Haley. He shouldered his shovel and stepped back. His friends followed, their blue, red, and black coats sharp against the white.

Haley settled her gloves more firmly on her fingers and pulled her coat tighter. She was already cold now that Maddox's warmth didn't surround her, but the scarf he insisted she keep helped shield her neck and throat. Once she had the heater going in the car, she'd be fine.

Maddox said nothing. He handed her into the driver's seat, his grip steady, then closed the door for her. He leaned down, resting his arms on the roof as Haley pulled on her seatbelt.

"Ready?" he asked.

Haley nodded. She waited for him to ask her to stay, at least to say he'd be sorry to see her go. Maybe ask if they could keep in touch, see each other again.

Maddox's eyes remained unreadable. He'd lost everyone he'd deeply loved, she understood, his parents, his fiancé. Aunt Jane was the exception, and someday, he'd lose her too.

Now Haley was leaving him. But Maddox had never said one word about loving her, one word about not wanting to say good-bye. Perhaps he was relieved to see her go—they'd avoid an awkward ending to a relationship that had barely started.

"Thanks, Maddox," Haley said. "You and Aunt Jane have been so nice to me."

Maddox's eyes flickered. "You're calling me *nice*? You must be getting frostbite. Start it up, sweetheart. The engine will need to warm a while."

Haley's throat tightened. She tried to ignore her hurt and push the button on her key fob to start the car.

The engine made a scraping sound, then fell silent. Haley clicked the fob again. Again, one cough, then nothing.

"Why don't you use the actual key?" Maddox asked impatiently.

Haley gave him an exasperated look. "I don't think it will make a difference." Her fingers were shaking so hard it took her three tries to slide the key into the slot.

She cranked, foot on the gas. Two coughs this time, then the engine quieted. Something hissed to the snow.

Maddox opened the door and jerked his thumb at her. "Out."

Haley scrambled up, Maddox helping her to her feet with breath-stealing strength. For a moment, his hands rested on her arms, his body close, his gaze holding hers. Then he gently set her aside and slid into her car, his large body dwarfing the small interior. He turned the key, pumped the gas, tried again.

Nothing. The car wheezed, then it threw up its metaphorical hands and surrendered.

Maddox climbed out, shaking his head. "Sitting out here exposed didn't do it any good. We can tow it to the house, get it into the garage, recharge the battery."

"This is a brand new car," Haley said in frustration. "It had ten miles on it when I drove it out of the dealership."

Maddox patted its top. "It's pretty." He slanted Haley a teasing look. "But I'd say you bought a lemon."

"A Mercedes S-class is not a lemon," she said hotly. "They are some of the best cars in the world."

"Nice for driving in the cushy city," Maddox said. "Not out here."

"I had no intention of *being* out here. I — Oh, never mind." Haley waved her hands in impatience. "I'm freezing. Can I sit in someone's truck?"

"No, I'll take you back home. Buddy will bring your car."

Sounded fine to Haley. She tried not to enjoy Maddox's warm hands on her waist as he lifted her to Sammy's saddle, the routine now familiar. Haley also liked the part when he put his foot in the stirrup and swung on behind her.

He snaked his arms around her, holding her close, while he turned Sammy toward the ranch.

The quiet ride was beautiful. Snow glittered where the sun broke through the clouds, the woods closing around them in shades of black, green, and white. When they came out of the trees to view the mountains lifting behind the house and barn, Haley's heart swelled with a kind of joy.

Aunt Jane waited on the porch. She hadn't bothered to put on a coat, but she didn't shiver, as though she didn't notice the cold. "Car wouldn't start?" she asked without surprise. "I expected as much."

"Sorry, Aunt Jane," Haley said as Maddox swung down and helped Haley to the ground. "Looks like I'll have to stay another night. It will be too far for me to start today even if someone can fix my car. It's eight hours from here to Seattle—and that's only if I don't stop for the bathroom."

"Of course, honey," Aunt Jane said. "But tomorrow's Christmas Eve. I doubt anyone will have time to get parts for your car until the twenty-sixth. And even if they did, you don't want to spend Christmas on the road."

"Then I'll rent or borrow a car," Haley said. "I'd rather reach home late and at least have dinner with my dad. I don't want him to be alone."

"I know, sweetie, but it's risky, and you need to be careful—"

Aunt Jane's words cut off as Maddox strode up to Haley, Sammy standing quietly where he'd been left. "If you want to be home in time for Christmas, Haley, *I'll* take you."

Haley turned to him, lips parting. "On Sammy?" she asked, the joke falling faintly.

"In my truck," Maddox replied in a hard voice. "If Buddy says he can get you to a highway, then he can get me there too. Easier in my truck anyway. That car you have is like a doll carriage."

Haley decided not to mention that the doll carriage was a hundred-thousand dollar vehicle. "But what about *your* Christmas? You can't leave Aunt Jane alone."

"Don't you worry about that," Maddox said firmly. "I'll be back in plenty of time."

"Can you trust a ranch truck to make it to a big city?" she countered, one hand on her hip.

"Sure can, darlin'. You grab your bags, and we'll go. Sooner we start, sooner I can get home again."

Aunt Jane already had Haley's suitcases and briefcase ready at the door. Maddox turned and strode to the garage, which rested a little way from the house.

Haley climbed the porch and hugged Aunt Jane, tears springing to her eyes. "Thank you for everything," she said.

Aunt Jane's eyes were moist as well. She patted Haley's back and held her close. "It was no problem, honey. I loved having you. Please say you'll come back."

She pulled away and looked at Haley in hope. Aunt Jane wanted her to stay with Maddox, Haley realized. Wanted them to be a couple.

Maddox had to want that too. Haley started to answer at the same time a roar came from the garage. What did he have in there, a dragon?

She hugged Aunt Jane again. "I'll try," she said. "I promise. But only if Maddox wants me to."

"He does," Aunt Jane said. "He won't tell you that, but I know."

"I *will* try," Haley repeated. "I like it here. I'd love to see it in the spring."

Aunt Jane nodded, wiping her eyes. "It's beautiful then."

She said the words wistfully—she didn't believe Haley would return.

The roar intensified. Sammy looked around but showed no signs of wanting to bolt. He simply watched as Maddox drove out of the garage.

Maddox's truck surprised Haley. Buddy and his friends had driven large monsters that were rusty from snow and salted roads. They might have powerful engines, but they were ratty-looking on the outside.

Maddox's truck was a little smaller, sleek, black, and gleaming. The cab was large, enough for several passengers, and the bed had a cover to keep whatever he hauled out of the weather.

He might have poked fun at Haley's car, but Maddox obviously took great care of his pickup. He went slowly around the drive, halting about ten yards from the porch.

The truck purred as he set the brake, the engine defiant of the cold. Maddox hopped out and opened the passenger door, indicating with a sweep of his arm that Haley should enter.

As Haley picked up her briefcase, Lance barreled out of the house, leapt into the cab, and settled himself on the bench seat in the back.

"Lance," Maddox admonished, but Aunt Jane shook her head.

"Take him with you, Maddox. He'll whine at me all day if you don't."

Maddox heaved a sigh but conceded. Lance, knowing he'd won, thumped his tail on the seat.

"Won't he have to eat and go to the bathroom?" Haley asked as Maddox stepped past her to grab her suitcases.

"I have food and dog bowls in the truck already," Maddox said. "Lance likes to go for rides, if you haven't guessed. Will your city folk faint if they see a Labrador in a truck?"

"Of course not. A lot of people in Seattle have dogs. Even big ones."

Maddox slanted her a *sure-they-do* look and tucked her suitcases next to Lance. Maddox snatched her briefcase, which had her phone in it, out of her hand and put it in the back as well. "No texting and driving," he admonished.

"But *you'll* be driving," Haley said with exaggerated patience.

"I know. But you texting while I'm driving will make me crazy. Get in."

Maddox helped her up into the truck the same way he did when he put her on Sammy—strength and agility, guiding her exactly where she needed to go. The powerful boost at the end slid her halfway across the seat.

"Be careful out there, Maddox," Aunt Jane said. "Don't worry about Sammy. I've got him."

"Sure thing, Aunt Jane. Be back before you know it."

Maddox slammed Haley's door then climbed into the driver's side and banged that door shut as well. The pickup was already toasty warm, Haley's fingers and nose quickly thawing.

Maddox must have called his friends as he readied the pickup, because Buddy and company appeared at the end of the driveway, their huge four-wheel drive trucks packing down the snow.

Maddox followed them out, the convoy slowly making their way under the arch that marked the entrance to Stardust Ranch, across a bridge that had been cleared of snow and ice, up a rise, and onward toward open country.

Haley looked back. Beyond the fold of hill where Maddox's ranch nestled, the lake stretched out in ice-blue glory, tiny buildings hugged its shore, and giant mountains framed the view.

Yes, she'd be back. Knowing this corner of the world existed, Haley would not be able to stay away. She'd return to Starlight Bend whether Maddox Campbell welcomed her or not.

BUDDY AND HIS FRIENDS PULLED ASIDE AT THE turnoff to the main highway, ten miles from Maddox's ranch. The highway had been plowed, the sides filled with steep banks of snow, but the road was at least drivable.

In fifty miles, Maddox would hit the interstate, and then it would be smooth sailing through Idaho and all the way across Washington. He waved his friends a thanks and turned onto the shining road.

Haley didn't say much beside him. This stretch of highway went through the reservation, quiet, smooth, empty. Haley looked around, taking in the hills, the wide sky, the mountains. Montana at its best.

Maddox remained silent as well. What was there to say? They'd made love—which had been the best of the best—but Haley had a life to go back to. So did Maddox. He had plenty to do, plenty of people and animals to take care of. Nothing empty about his life.

Haley would make no promises. Neither would Maddox.

They reached the I-90. The freeway was clear and nearly dry from sunshine and traffic. Several eighteen-wheelers passed, mud flaps flying, the last moving over so Maddox could merge onto the road.

He put his foot down on the gas. With any luck, they'd make Seattle before ten tonight, and Haley would get her Christmas Eve with her dad.

He knew she'd try to find Maddox someplace to

sleep so he could drive back in the early hours and make it in time for Christmas with Aunt Jane and all the people she'd invited. Aunt Jane opened their home every year to those who might not have anyone to be with or the means for a decent Christmas, as well as family and friends. Christmas dinners overflowed the house with laughter, good times, and gratitude.

They passed a town called Riverbend, which always made Maddox smile—his cousins lived in a town of the same name down in Texas. Their Riverbend lay in the rolling hills outside Austin—this one was in a cut of the mountains, following a river valley, miles from any big city.

The freeway curved and swayed around snowy mountains rising to either side of the road. More traffic here, people hurrying home for Christmas or heading to the ski resorts to spend the holiday there.

Lookout Pass, which lay on the border between Idaho and Montana, was coming up fast. Signs for the turnoff and ski areas flashed by, then they passed a big blue one that read, "Welcome to Idaho."

*I'm going to tell her,* Maddox said silently. *I'm going to tell her that I'm staying with her for Christmas Eve, meeting her dad. And then she's coming back to Starlight Bend with me, and we're going to see if we have something. No ships passing in the night. No fading memory of a wild one-night stand. I don't want to live the rest of my life not knowing if we could have had a future.*

*I don't want country-western songs. I want real life. I want Haley.*

Behind him, Lance stirred and started to pant.

"Haley," Maddox began in a firm voice.

At the same time, Haley shouted, "Maddox! Stop!"

## Chapter Eleven

✦

Maddox kept himself from slamming on the brakes. On a wintery road with a six percent downgrade and semis whizzing past, that was a bad idea.

His hands shook but he made himself move down the road, passing runaway truck ramps until he reached an exit. He slid the truck down the exit ramp, found a spot to pull over on the road at the bottom, and stopped.

He turned to Haley. Her eyes were wide, breath coming fast. She had one hand braced on the dashboard as though trying to stop the pickup with sheer willpower.

"You all right, sweetheart?" Maddox asked her in consternation. "What's wrong?"

"Turn around," Haley said, her eyes glittering with tears. "We have to go back."

"Why? Did you forget something?" *Don't tell me it's her laptop or something stupid like that.*

"My wish!"

"What?" Maddox stared at her, gripping the wheel. "What are you talking about?" Lance perked up and watched, interested.

"My wish — Santa said it had come true. No, he said ..." Haley fished around in her pocket and drew out a card edged with red gilt. "It says, *Your Wish Has Been Granted.*" She gave him a round-eyed look over the card. "I have to go back to Starlight Bend."

Maddox's heartbeat sped, his fingers tingling with sudden heat. He wanted with everything in him to drive this truck back to the freeway and point it east. But he sat still.

"Tell me what in hell you're going on about."

Haley's eyes began to shine. "I was stuck, my car wouldn't start, the phones didn't work, my dad told me I needed to stay, even Lance didn't want me leaving without him. And Santa told me — a guy who looks just like the real Santa Claus — that what I'd wished for had already come true. Don't you see? It's me in Starlight Bend ... with *you.*"

*Hell yes, with me!*

Maddox couldn't make his lips move to say the words. His mouth was dry and cottony, his throat shut tight.

"Santa ..." he forced out with a croak. Behind him, Lance whined.

Haley's smile died. "But only if you want me to."

This was it—Maddox's opportunity to make his big speech.

*Stay with me, Haley. Forever. Not star-crossed lovers but lovers under the stars in Big Sky Country. I don't want you just for Christmas, but for always.*

No way could his tongue get out something so schmaltzy.

"Haley." Maddox's voice was hoarse. He cleared his throat. And again. Damn it, he should have brought some water with him.

Maddox coughed one more time and started to speak.

An eighteen-wheeler rumbled by, engine-braking with a roar, the driver honking in irritation at Maddox's truck on the side of the road. Maddox's words were drowned even as they came out.

"What?" Haley asked over the noise.

"I said— *Will you marry me*?" Maddox shouted.

The passing truck's racket died after his preliminary words, and *Will you marry me?* rang loudly through the pickup. Lance barked.

Haley sat with her mouth hanging open, her red lips moist, enticing Maddox to kiss her.

To hell with it. Maddox ripped off his seatbelt, slid himself across to Haley, wrapped his arms around her, and dragged her up to him.

Just before their lips touched, Haley said, "Yes."

Maddox drew back. "What?"

Haley sat up. In a voice as loud as Maddox's, she yelled, "Yes, I will marry you!"

Maddox thumped back in his seat. *"Shit."*

"What's the matter?" Haley's eyes lit. "Want to take it back?"

"Hell no!" Maddox pounded his hands on the steering wheel. "I just realized I proposed to you in a pickup on the side of the road with the dog drooling in my back seat."

Lance barked twice.

"I know," Haley said. She laughed. "It's perfect."

Maddox wasted no more time with words. He moved to Haley, hauled her into his arms, and brought his mouth down on hers.

The kiss heated his blood and the air around them, sound rushing in his ears. Haley tasted of desire and goodness, of love and excitement. Her body was hot against his, the softness of her a sharp contrast to the hard edges of his life.

Haley kissed him back with enthusiasm, her lips lush, the seatbelt between them not getting in her way. She swept her tongue into his mouth, the little noises in her throat reminding him of the sounds she'd made when he'd thrust into her on her bed.

His cock was rising, remembering it too. Even the seatbelt buckle digging into this hipbone couldn't stop the rush of hunger for her.

Another eighteen-wheeler rolled by, going the other way, this one honking repeatedly. The driver rolled down his window and yelled out, "Woo hoo! Merry Christmas! Go for it, man!"

Haley broke from Maddox, blushing furiously.

Maddox's face ached, and he realized he was smiling hard. He gave a thumb's up to the passing truck, and the driver honked as he fishtailed around the corner.

"Guess we should go," Maddox said, forcing himself back to his seat.

"Yes, I guess we should." Haley laughed, a sound like chimes in the Christmas air. "Please, Maddox. Take me home."

———

THE PIES HAD BEEN BAKED, THE TURKEY READY and waiting in the fridge, the last decorations put on the tree. Boxes wrapped, bows tied, Lance running around with a big jingle bell attached to his collar.

Haley, Maddox, and Aunt Jane had made their careful way to church for a Christmas Eve service, back for dinner, and then to bed.

As Haley lay in the small bedroom, her body wrapped around Maddox's larger one, snowflakes drifted past the window.

On the rug, Lance began to snore. In the bed, Maddox did too.

Haley laughed softly. "I love you, Maddox Campbell."

Maddox's eyes cracked open instantly. He'd either been faking, or the words had dragged him out of his dreams.

A slow smile spread across his face. "I love *you*, Haley McKee. Merry Christmas."

"Merry Christmas," Haley whispered back.

Lance drew a long breath and heaved it out in vast contentment.

"'And to all a good night,'" Haley said.

"Night's still young." Maddox's voice held a sinful note.

"That's a good point." Haley laughed up at him as his mouth came down on hers, and he loved her again, very early on a snowy Christmas morning.

The best Christmas present ever. Santa had been right—what Haley had wished for in her heart had indeed come true.

# Epilogue

F rom Danny Vining, Starlight Bend, Montana, to
Santa Claus, The North Pole
Dear Santa,

Thank you for giving me the best Christmas ever.
Maddox Campbell took me over to Oregon to see my dad.
Maddox stayed with me the whole way, even the scary part
in the prison, waiting with all the other kids to see
their dads.

I was afraid I wouldn't know what to say, because I
hadn't seen Dad in so long. I was really little when he
went away.

But when I spotted him in the room waiting for us, I
didn't worry anymore. They let me go right up to him, so I
ran to him and hugged him hard.

Dad hugged me back, and he started crying. I asked him
what was wrong, and he said he was crying because he was
happy.

He said thank you to Maddox for bringing me to see

him. *Maddox said no, it was Haley that made it happen, and told Dad he was going to marry Haley, who is very pretty. Dad said, Good for you, and tell her thank you.*

Then he asked about Mom. Mom hadn't wanted to come, and Dad said he understood. He'd done a bad thing leaving her, but he regretted it, and hoped that when he finished paying for what he'd done — he'd robbed a store so he could buy more alcohol, he told me straight out, and told me it was the worst mistake he'd made in his life. Maybe someday he could go apologize to Mom and see if they could at least be friends again.

I told him I'd talk to her, and he laughed. Then he hugged me again and asked me to tell him everything.

Maddox sat with us, and I told Dad things that had happened at home since I'd seen him. Maddox seemed surprised I had so much to say, because I don't talk much around him. That's not because I don't want to, but I figure no one is interested in what I want to talk about. Dad wanted to hear everything.

I had to leave too soon, but Dad said I could come back anytime. Maddox promised to bring me, said he'd set up a schedule. I didn't tell Dad, but I decided I'd talk to Mom and see if she'd start coming with me. Maybe not next time, but when she was ready.

I hugged and kissed Dad good-bye, and then Maddox took me out. He and Haley are getting married in January, and they already invited me to the wedding. I will take lots of pictures and show them to Dad.

So, thank you, Santa. I knew you wouldn't let me down. I know Maddox and Haley set it up, but they couldn't have *without you. Haley even helped me with this letter to you, making sure I spelled everything right. She's a nice lady.*

*Stay warm at the North Pole. Maddox says it's even colder there than in Montana, and we're pretty cold here.*

*Talk to you next year.*

*Love,*

*Danny*

---

*ONE YEAR LATER*

"JUST ABOUT DONE." MADDOX HUNG AN ornament in the shape of Seattle's Space Needle near the top of the tree, and looked at his work with satisfaction.

"It could use more." Haley sat behind him on the sofa, among tissue paper, lights, and more ornaments than any man could get on a tree of any size. If Maddox put on everything Haley and Aunt Jane wanted, he wouldn't be done decorating until April.

"I want it perfect for Dad," Haley said, lifting her head to look at Maddox.

Maddox fell in love with her all over again.

His wife's honey-colored hair was caught in a simple ponytail, and she wore jeans and a sweater, long ago adopting clothes more suited to living on a ranch where summers were cool and winter snows were deep. Haley caught his stare with her brown eyes and flashed him a smile.

She was the most beautiful thing he'd ever seen.

Maddox tapped the ornament, a souvenir from their last visit to Seattle, descended the ladder, and crossed the living room to her. Haley's face softened as Maddox leaned down and gently kissed her mouth.

Sweet, warm Haley. She laced her arms around Maddox's neck and pulled him close, opening her lips to kiss him fully. Her sweater hugged her chest, letting Maddox feel the woman inside as he slid his hand down to cup her breast.

Hot breath touched his thigh, then a pile of fur pushed between himself and Haley, along with the smell of snowy dog. Haley laughed as the kiss broke, and she bent to Lance, rubbing his body and resting her cheek on the top of his head.

"Great timing, my friend," Maddox growled.

Lance panted up at him, looking smug. Sure he was. Haley was now all over *him*.

Since February, when Haley and Maddox had returned from their honeymoon in the sunshine of Maui, Haley had been working her job online, telecommuting to her father's business. They'd set up an office for her in one of the upstairs bedrooms, and she travelled to Seattle from time to time to meet with her father and other executives. Or her father and colleagues came here. Starlight Bend in the summer was a beautiful place, and more fishing got done than working.

Maddox, unused to hot climates, hadn't thought he'd like Hawaii, but he'd found ranchers there who were as willing to fling back a beer and chew the fat as his cronies in Starlight Bend. He'd made friends with the ranchers, discussing the differences between running cattle in cold country and warm, though it snowed on the tops of the high volcanoes on the Big Island. He talked horses with Hawaiians while Haley looked sexy in her bathing suit at the beach, adorable in her snorkel gear.

The nights in their retreat on the secluded side of Maui made Maddox realize he might not mind a wife with money. The romantic hideaway where they could make love all night in the moonlight or lie back listening to the rain was worth it.

Outside, a car door slammed. Lance squirted out from Haley's embrace and headed for the front door, which he shoved open, letting in a blast of freezing air.

"It's Dad!" Haley jumped to her feet, scattering lights and paper garlands, her eyes starry. "Lance must have come to tell us he's here."

She caught Maddox's hand and dragged him behind her on the way out the door, not stopping for a coat or gloves. She stomped down the porch stairs in her boots, flinging out her sweatered arms to grab her father in a fervent embrace.

Robert McKee had silver hair, a trim body, and

Haley's brown eyes. He caught his daughter up and swung her around, both of them laughing as he set her on her feet.

Robert came forward, his arm outstretched, as Maddox reached them. He shook Maddox's hand in a grip that was firm but not harsh. Maddox had realized his strength when they'd first met, just before the wedding. He'd also realized that he liked Robert McKee, who was quiet, thoughtful, and considerate to others, something Maddox hadn't expected from a rich corporate man. He'd rearranged his prejudices a lot since meeting Haley's family.

"How are you, Maddox?" Robert asked with enthusiasm. "Is she taking care of you all right?"

"Oh, she's muddling through," Maddox said with a shrug.

Haley rolled her eyes at both of them and started for the house. Aunt Jane intercepted them on the porch.

"I've never met a man who was so punctual," Aunt Jane said crisply. "Must be a record. I've got supper ready to serve, but you have time to wash up first."

Robert rubbed his gloved hands. "I've been thinking about Jane Howard's delicious steak and potatoes all the way from Seattle. Made me break all kinds of speed limit laws."

Aunt Jane was pleased but strove to hide it. "Leave the suitcases for now. Maddox will grab them after dinner."

"Yes, ma'am," Robert said. "Hello, Lance. How are you, old buddy?" He leaned down and half hugged Lance, patting his sides with as much enthusiasm as Haley did. Lance loved it, wagging his tail so hard his entire body moved, as did Robert's.

Robert straightened up and headed inside. His eyes met Aunt Jane's on the way and his face softened as he smiled just a little bit. Aunt Jane—severe Aunt Jane—flushed a carnation pink, but gazed right back at him.

Robert disappeared inside and Aunt Jane followed, giving him directions to the bathroom, even though he already knew where it was.

Maddox gestured for Haley to precede him into the warm house, but she hung back and clutched his sleeve. "Did you see that?" she whispered.

"Yep. Also saw it last time he visited."

Haley started to glare, then the glare vanished. "Yeah, I did too." She looked thoughtful. "Hmm."

She started in after Aunt Jane, but Maddox pulled her back to the doorway, above which mistletoe had been nailed. "We should let them work it out for themselves."

"Like we did?" Haley's eyes glinted with humor. "'Cause we did so well. It almost didn't happen, we're both so stubborn."

"Hey, we're here, aren't we?" Maddox pulled her closer. The cold didn't push at him with Haley against his body. He gave her a leisurely kiss, brushing her soft lips, liking how her lashes swept down as she kissed him back.

"Yes," Haley said softly. "We're here. I wouldn't be anywhere else."

"Miss the big city?" Maddox's heart beat faster as he waited for her answer. Haley had seemed happy here for the last year, but he'd never pressed the question.

"Sometimes." Haley's breath brushed his lips. "But that's what cars and airplanes are for. I can visit anytime I want, though I don't seem to want to as much as I thought I would."

Maddox nodded. "Montana grows on you."

"No, *you* grow on me." Haley grinned. "I want to be where you are, Maddox. Always."

Maddox tried to think of a smart-ass comeback to continue their smart-ass comeback competition, but nothing sprang to his lips. He only wanted to kiss Haley again.

He scooped her to him to take her mouth. Haley's fire heated his blood, and the scrape of her teeth on his lips made him wish dinner was a long way off. His wife was one hell of a good kisser, and Maddox wanted to savor her all night.

He eased away and cupped her cheek. "Come on. Let's pretend we don't notice them making sheep's eyes at each other."

Haley laughed. "This should be fun."

Maddox gripped her elbow and guided her in, shutting out the cold for the warmth of his home.

AFTER DINNER, SNOW BEGAN TO FALL, WHICH grew thicker and heavier the darker the night became. Robert offered to help Aunt Jane wash up so the newlyweds could enjoy snuggling by the fire. Maddox and Haley exchanged a surreptitious, knowing look.

Later, when they sought their bed in the large front bedroom they'd moved into, Maddox moved into Haley's warmth, kissing her hair, her neck, letting his hands wander her bare body. "Heard we'll be snowed in by morning."

Haley made a noise of pleasure low in her throat. "No bad thing. Being snowbound is fun—when you're snowbound with the right person."

"Damn straight. You're the right one for me, Haley Campbell."

"You know you are for me. Or else I wouldn't have made you stop in the middle of nowhere and propose to me."

"Is that what you did?" He kissed her breast then circled her nipple with his tongue. "I thought getting married was my idea."

"It was *our* idea." Haley touched his face, and when he raised his head, she pulled him in for a deep kiss.

"I like that," he said when he finished.

She gave him a sly look. "I might as well give you your Christmas present now."

"Mmm, and I like the sound of *that*." Maddox started to kiss her again, positioning her so he could slide inside her.

Haley put her hands on his chest. "You don't know what it is, yet."

"No?" Maddox raised his brows. "I thought you were giving me *you*."

"That's not just for Christmas." Haley blushed hard as soon as the words came out, as though she hadn't meant to say it like that. "You know what I mean."

Maddox chuckled. "Yeah, I do, and I'm enjoying it."

Haley pushed at him before he could kiss her. "The present is—next year we'll need to convert another bedroom. And we'll have a bigger gathering at Christmas."

Maddox frowned a moment, and then his heart gave one big *bang* as his body registered what she meant before his brain caught up.

"Are you fucking kidding me?" The words were a croak. "You're— We—" As usual, his throat squeezed shut when it was time to say the most important things.

"Yes, I'm ... We are ..." Haley touched his lips. "Having a baby."

"Holy *shit*."

Maddox stared at his beautiful wife as incredible waves of happiness spilled over him.

He was going to be a dad. With Haley, the

woman he loved more than his own life. Their love had only deepened and grown in the last year, from a bright opening spark to a long-burning flame. And now it would grow, and grow. Maddox drew a ragged breath, barely able to take in the news.

Haley frowned. "Maddox? You okay?"

Maddox let out the breath in one explosive exhale. "Hell yes, I'm okay. I'm all kinds of okay. Son of a bitch! That's one hell of a Christmas gift. The best one I ever got—well, except for you saying you'd marry me."

Haley looked relieved. "Good. For a second I thought you were upset."

"Upset? What the hell would I be upset about? I love kids, and I'll love *this* kid." Maddox's face ached with his big smile as he slid his hand to her belly. "Love her—or him—like I love her—or his—mama."

Haley laughed in delight. "We'll have to find out which it is so you'll be able to talk coherently."

"I don't care. I'll love him—or her—I'm not bothered which." Maddox repressed the urge to spring out of bed and run around shouting by holding Haley tight. "I love you Haley Campbell."

"I love you, Maddox Campbell." Haley touched the bridge of his nose. "I think we should be snow-bound every Christmas."

"I'll arrange it." He didn't care if it snowed or not —he'd lock them in the house and make love to her until spring.

Haley rose up and kissed him, wrapping him in her arms and pulling him down to her warmth. Her love for him closed around Maddox, and he loved her in return, sliding his hands over her beautiful body before he sought the heat inside her.

They loved each other as snow whispered against the window, the quiet of the night settling peace in Maddox's soul, love in his heart. He looked into Haley's eyes, and surrendered to the magic.

# Author's Note

Thank you for reading! *Snowbound in Starlight Bend* is loosely connected to my Riding Hard series, about Maddox's cousins who are stunt riders in Hill Country, Texas—five brothers who are hard-riding and tender-loving.

For more information about that series and others, visit my website at http://www.jenniferashley.com. There you can sign up for my newsletter to be kept up to date on all my new releases, or join here: http://eepurl.com/47kLL

You can also follow me on Facebook (http://www.facebook.com/jenniferashleyallysonjam esashleygardner) and Twitter (http://www.twitter.com/JennAllyson)

Best Christmas wishes,

*Jennifer Ashley*

A dam heard himself flatline. The machine shrilled one long sound, and everything he'd ever known vanished. He saw no light, felt nothing; he had no body, did not exist.

There had been a roar, red fire, the stunt crew yelling, his best friend trapped in a pickup, surrounded by flame, eyes fixed in an unseeing stare. Then paramedics, fire trucks, noise, smoke, something jammed to Adam's face. And then nothing except lying motionless while the machine sang out that Adam Campbell was dead.

Next to his bed, a woman was crying. Couldn't be his mother; she never cried when things were bad. She'd get through it and then go to pieces later, like she'd done when his dad had died.

Dad had been about thirty-two when he'd passed —Adam was four years younger than that. *Sorry, Dad, meant to take care of them a little longer.*

Bright, hot fire blasted through Adam's body, streaking along every nerve. Adam's legs jerked, his fingers burned, pain seared through his chest to shoot upwards into his brain. *What the f—?*

He slammed back down on the bed, gasping for air. Cold and dry, it grated into his lungs. The machines stopped their long scream and started a rhythm, soft signals that overlapped one another and pulsed like his heart.

*Beat* … pause … *beat* … pause …

A very long time later, Adam peeled open his eyes.

They surrounded his bed, his mom flanked by four big, tough-looking men — Tyler, Grant, Ross, and Carter. Carter's large hand rested on the shoulder of his eight-year-old daughter, Faith's hazel eyes enormous in her small face.

His family had come all the way from Riverbend to watch him die.

"Hey," Adam croaked. His throat was raw with serious pain, his voice barely audible. "I feel like shit."

His younger brothers, Faith, and his mother relaxed into wide smiles—except for Carter, who'd never caught on to what smiling was all about. But even Carter's eyes warmed, the hand on Faith's shoulder easing.

For some reason, they were all very, very happy with Adam.

BAILEY WATCHED THE FAMILY DRIVE IN. SHE remained in the big corral, with Dodie on the other end of the longe line, teaching the horse to master her latest tricks for the upcoming movie shoot.

"You're supposed to be afraid," Bailey told the chocolate-brown horse waiting patiently for her cue. "Not enjoying it. No one's going to buy that."

Dodie reared up when Bailey gave the signal, pawing the air, then came down and danced aside, shuddering. Perfect shot—that should have been a take—but Dodie looked, well, *smug*. Bailey refused to actually scare a horse to make the trick work—no one on the Circle C Ranch was cruel to horses—so this was the best it was going to get. If the camera caught Dodie's movements and edited out that the mare was overacting, it should work.

A black SUV and two pickups rolled to the house on the rise, the family climbing out. Bailey moved to the rail to watch.

The entire Campbell family had flown to L.A. when word had come that Adam had been pulled out of the burning wreckage of a movie stunt gone wrong, barely alive. He was an experienced stuntman, but Adam performed some of the most dangerous feats in the business, and accidents happened.

Adam's mom had stayed out there with him for a few weeks while he began his healing, his brothers going back and forth, but they'd all congregated today to bring him home from the airport in Austin.

Bailey's heart had dropped like a stone when she'd heard about Adam's accident. Olivia Campbell, Adam's mother and Bailey's current employer, had asked Bailey if she'd like to come with them, knowing Bailey and Adam had once been close. Bailey had declined, though it had taken all her resolve to not rush to his bedside. She knew the family would want to be together if they lost him, no outsiders.

Whether Adam made it or not, Bailey didn't trust herself not to betray her feelings. She and Adam had led very different lives since age eighteen, when they'd both left the small town of Riverbend, Texas, to go their separate ways—he to Hollywood to wrangle horses and ride in movies; Bailey to Austin and UT.

They'd parted as friends, each moving on to other relationships, but when Bailey had heard the news that Adam might not survive, she'd realized that, in her heart, it had always been Adam.

Bailey stilled as she caught sight of Adam in the passenger seat. The longe line went slack, and Dodie joined Bailey at the fence, the horse watching with her.

Adam was helped out of the truck by Grant on one side, Carter on the other. Small Faith moved like a satellite between them, her hands out as though ready to catch her uncle Adam in case he slipped.

Bailey saw Adam make a curt gesture at his brothers as he adjusted his crutches. She could guess what he was saying: *Don't baby me. I'm older than you.*

Dodie, recognizing the family, let out a throaty neigh of welcome.

Every single one of them turned and looked down to the corrals. Tyler and Grant waved, and Bailey lifted her hand in return.

Faith made a gesture to Adam, as though telling him not to fall while she was gone, and broke away toward Bailey. She pranced to the corral in her imitation of a horse's canter, and Dodie's ears pricked.

Now Adam was looking down the slope. He raised a hand to shade his eyes. *Who is that?* he'd be asking.

One of his brothers, probably Grant, the second-oldest Campbell, would answer. *Your ex. She works for us now.*

Grant liked to teasingly call Bailey "Adam's Ex." A year younger than Adam, Grant had been a good friend the few weeks Bailey and Adam had gone out.

At the time, Bailey had kept Adam from flunking out of school by helping him through the last of his exams so he could stand up and graduate with his class. They'd had a small, intense fling—the kind you have when you're young and poised on the edge of adulthood—then they'd gone their separate ways. No recriminations, no hurting. They'd both been ready to get on with their lives.

*Who am I kidding?* Bailey had told herself, when Adam was offered the chance to take his riding skills to Hollywood, that her rosy dreams of marrying him and settling down had been just that, dreams. Not reality.

Bailey had accepted a scholarship to the University of Texas in Austin and started her own life, quickly earning a bachelor's then a master's degree in math and computer science, working as a programmer in a large tech company after that. Interesting projects, long hours, lots of money, a new kind of crowd, a three-year marriage, and a divorce.

When she'd discovered the true nature of her cheating husband, and the lack of loyalty among their friends, she'd quit her antacid-popping job and returned to her roots in the little town of Riverbend, in the heart of Hill Country. She'd asked Olivia Campbell and her sons, the best stunt trainers in the business, for a job. Bailey might be a math geek, but she'd grown up with horses and knew how to bring out the best in them.

The Campbells, along with their foster brother, Carter Sullivan, were stunt riders and horse trainers, their talents highly sought after, their acts popular at rodeos and exhibitions throughout Texas. Adam had been snatched up to work full-time on movies by California studios, while the other brothers were wranglers and horse stunt riders for small-studio movies, television, and commercials throughout Texas and New Mexico.

Bailey knew when she came home that she didn't want to work anywhere else. Her stress levels had gone way down in the last year—she'd arrived burned out and defeated, and now she slept like a baby. The Campbells had offered Bailey a refuge, and she'd taken it.

And now Adam was home.

The brothers were pretending not to hover around him, but they surrounded Adam like bodyguards as he hobbled onto the porch and finally dropped into a waiting chair. The crutches that had held him up clattered to the wooden porch floor.

Adam irritably waved off his brothers as they stooped to retrieve the crutches, and again, Bailey imagined what he was saying: *Stop fussing and grab me a beer.*

Bailey saw Olivia shake her head and Adam flop his hands to the arms of the chair in resignation. Probably he couldn't have any alcohol on whatever meds he was on.

Olivia would offer him her famous iced tea now —not sweet tea, which Adam didn't like. Adam gave a nod, and Olivia walked into the house.

From this angle, Bailey could see through the window into the living room. Olivia was heading to the kitchen, wiping her eyes.

Faith reached the corral. She was horse-wise enough to stop fluttering around once near Dodie, but she was still excited.

Faith addressed Dodie first. "I don't have any

treats for you," she said as the mare lowered her nose to Faith's hands. "But if you're good, I'll sneak you some tortilla chips later. You know she really likes those," Faith said to Bailey.

Six months ago, when Dodie'd had the horse equivalent of a bad cold, the only things she would eat were tortilla chips and pizza. Faith was convinced they'd saved her life.

"Uncle Adam growled all the way from Austin," Faith said. "He growled on the plane from L.A. too. He is *not* a good patient, Grandma says."

"Can't blame him." Bailey observed the brothers trying to make their oldest sibling comfortable. "The wreck was really bad."

"A truck crashed into his motorcycle then Uncle Adam and the truck smashed into a building that fell down on them, and the pickup blew up. For real. The other stuntman died, and Uncle Adam is really upset about it. He doesn't say that, but we can tell."

Bailey had heard details of the accident from Olivia and Grant, but Faith's matter-of-fact summation made her heart constrict. "It's terrible. I'm so sorry."

"Uncle Adam broke a lot of bones, and his face is all burned, but his injuries weren't as bad as they could have been, the doctors told us. Uncle Adam's mad—not that he was hurt, but that nothing more happened to him. He keeps saying *Dawson died, and all I got was a broken leg and a sissy burn.*"

Bailey's hand tightened on the longe line until her knuckles hurt. "Poor Adam."

Adam Campbell didn't like to show his emotions. He'd be gruff and growling, all the while his heart was breaking. Bailey had seen that in him before, and she didn't like that it was happening again.

"We feel bad for him," Faith said, in her clear-eyed way. "But he doesn't want us feeling bad, so that makes him angry too. It's complicated, Dad says."

Faith's dad was Carter Sullivan, whose life had been extremely complicated before Olivia had brought him here to foster him.

"I guess we have to let him heal," Bailey said. She leaned her arms on the top rail of the corral and gazed at Adam on the porch, surrounded by tall Campbell men.

Dodie stretched her neck down to Faith again, so Faith could keep petting her. All the horses liked Faith, except for Buster, but he was a crabby old fart who hated everybody.

"I guess," Faith said. "Grandma says, do you want to stay for dinner?"

Up at the house, the brothers were dropping away from Adam, one by one, to unload the SUV, to go inside and help Olivia, or head to the barn to help settle the horses for the night. Adam remained in the chair, alone, giving Bailey a clear view of him.

He sat there, exhausted, broken, and Bailey's heart squeezed again. Adam had always been so *alive*. Being with him had been like holding a lit firework. He'd had a restless energy that could fuel a rocket, and a smile that lit up the sky.

Now he sat, head back, body still. Adam Campbell never, ever sat still.

As though he sensed her, Adam raised his head and looked down the hill.

Bailey could feel his intense blue gaze, those eyes framed with the blackest lashes she'd ever seen. His hair wasn't black, it was dark brown—when they'd been kids, it had always been burned with blond streaks. These days he wore it short, and the streaks weren't as obvious, but the short cut revealed every line of his handsome face.

Now that face was burned and scarred, she'd heard from Grant, though she couldn't see it from here. Beautiful Adam used to have every girl in town quivering when he walked by. Even ones who considered themselves too sophisticated for a local cowboy had turned their heads to watch him pass. They'd made sure their breasts turned in his direction too, and Adam hadn't been oblivious.

Bailey had gone a lot further with him than those girls ever dreamed—but that was a long time ago.

"Not sure it's a good idea," Bailey said in answer to Faith's offer of supper. "I don't want to make Adam self-conscious."

"Oh, come on, Bailey, *pleeeze*? He'll want to see you. I know all about you and Adam in the old days —Dad told me. Adam's still in love with you."

Bailey looked at her in alarm. "Adam told you that, did he?"

"He doesn't have to tell me," Faith said, stroking Dodie's neck. "I *know*."

Sweet of her, but Bailey wasn't stupid. There had been too many years, too many differences in their lives, to think anything she'd kindled with Adam in high school would remain. He'd recover from his injuries and return to Hollywood, and Bailey would stay here, working with the Campbells, enjoying the unhurried pace of her life.

That was how it would be.

"Okay, Bailey?" Faith said. "You're staying, right?"

Bailey sighed as she unhooked the longe line from Dodie and started winding it up. She'd have to face Adam sometime, and it might as well be now as later. They'd get the awkwardness out of the way then go on with their lives until he left again.

"All right," she told Faith. "Help me put away Dodie, and I'll stay for dinner."

"Woot!" Faith climbed through the bars and easily caught sweet-tempered Dodie by the halter. Bailey snapped on the lead rope, and Faith happily led Dodie to her stall as the sun sank behind the hill, everything good in the little girl's world.

Tiger Magic

Feral Heat

Wild Wolf

Bear Attraction

Mate Bond

Lion Eyes

Bad Wolf

Wild Things

White Tiger

Guardian's Mate

Red Wolf

Midnight Wolf

Tiger Striped

(novella)

Shifter Made ("Prequel" short story)

## Immortals
## (Paranormal Romance)

The Calling (by Jennifer Ashley)

The Darkening (by Robin Popp)

The Awakening (by Joy Nash)

The Gathering (by Jennifer Ashley)

The Redeeming (by Jennifer Ashley)

The Crossing (by Joy Nash)

The Haunting (by Robin Popp)

Blood Debt (by Joy Nash)

Wolf Hunt (by Jennifer Ashley)

Forbidden Taste (by Jennifer Ashley)

**Stormwalker**

**(Paranormal Romance**

**w/a Allyson James)**

Stormwalker

Firewalker

Shadow Walker

"Double Hexed"

Nightwalker

Dreamwalker

Dragon Bites

**Historical Romances**

**The Mackenzies Series**

The Madness of Lord Ian Mackenzie

Lady Isabella's Scandalous Marriage

The Many Sins of Lord Cameron

The Duke's Perfect Wife

A Mackenzie Family Christmas: The Perfect Gift

The Seduction of Elliot McBride

The Untamed Mackenzie

The Wicked Deeds of Daniel Mackenzie

Scandal and the Duchess

Rules for a Proper Governess

The Stolen Mackenzie Bride

A Mackenzie Clan Gathering

Alec Mackenzie's Art of Seduction

The Devilish Lord Will

**Nvengaria Series**

*(paranormal historical)*

Penelope & Prince Charming

The Mad, Bad Duke

Highlander Ever After

The Longest Night

**Regency Pirate Series**

The Pirate Next Door

The Pirate Hunter

The Care and Feeding of Pirates

# About the Author

*New York Times* bestselling and award-winning author Jennifer Ashley has written more than 85 published novels and novellas in romance, urban fantasy, and mystery under the names Jennifer Ashley, Allyson James, and Ashley Gardner. Her books have been nominated for and won Romance Writers of America's RITA (given for the best romance novels and novellas of the year), several *RT BookReviews* Reviewers Choice awards (including Best Urban Fantasy, Best Historical Mystery, and Career Achievement in Historical Romance), and Prism awards for her paranormal romances. Jennifer's books have been translated into more than a dozen languages and have earned starred reviews in *Booklist*.

More about the Jennifer's books can be found at http://www.jenniferashley.com. Or join her newsletter at http://eepurl.com/47kLL

Made in the USA
Monee, IL
06 October 2023